The Sacre̱ ̱ ̱ ̱ ̱ ̱

(Relic Hunters #13)

By
David Leadbeater

Copyright © 2025 by David Leadbeater

ISBN: 9798283895673

All rights reserved.
No part of this publication may be reproduced, distributed, or transmitted in any form or by any means, including photocopying, recording, or other electronic or mechanical methods, without the prior written permission of the publisher/author except in the case of brief quotations embodied in critical reviews and certain other non-commercial uses permitted by copyright law.
All characters in this book are fictitious, and any resemblance to actual persons living or dead is purely coincidental.

This ebook is for your personal enjoyment only. This ebook may not be re-sold or given away to other people. If you would like to share this ebook with another person, please purchase any additional copy for each reader. If you're reading this book and did not purchase it, or it was not purchased for your use only, then please return it and purchase your own copy. Thank you for respecting the hard work of this author.

Classification: Thriller, adventure, action, mystery, suspense, archaeological, military, historical, assassination, terrorism, assassin, spy

Other Books by David Leadbeater:

Blood Requiem

The Matt Drake Series
A constantly evolving, action-packed romp based in the escapist action-adventure genre:

The Bones of Odin (Matt Drake #1)
The Blood King Conspiracy (Matt Drake #2)
The Gates of Hell (Matt Drake 3)
The Tomb of the Gods (Matt Drake #4)
Brothers in Arms (Matt Drake #5)
The Swords of Babylon (Matt Drake #6)
Blood Vengeance (Matt Drake #7)
Last Man Standing (Matt Drake #8)
The Plagues of Pandora (Matt Drake #9)
The Lost Kingdom (Matt Drake #10)
The Ghost Ships of Arizona (Matt Drake #11)
The Last Bazaar (Matt Drake #12)
The Edge of Armageddon (Matt Drake #13)
The Treasures of Saint Germain (Matt Drake #14)
Inca Kings (Matt Drake #15)
The Four Corners of the Earth (Matt Drake #16)
The Seven Seals of Egypt (Matt Drake #17)
Weapons of the Gods (Matt Drake #18)
The Blood King Legacy (Matt Drake #19)
Devil's Island (Matt Drake #20)
The Fabergé Heist (Matt Drake #21)
Four Sacred Treasures (Matt Drake #22)
The Sea Rats (Matt Drake #23)
Blood King Takedown (Matt Drake #24)
Devil's Junction (Matt Drake #25)
Voodoo soldiers (Matt Drake #26)
The Carnival of Curiosities (Matt Drake #27)
Theatre of War (Matt Drake #28)

Shattered Spear (Matt Drake #29)
Ghost Squadron (Matt Drake #30)
A Cold Day in Hell (Matt Drake #31)
The Winged Dagger (Matt Drake #32)
Two Minutes to Midnight (Matt Drake #33)
The Devil's Reaper (Matt Drake#34)
The Dark Tsar (Matt Drake #35)
The Hellhound Scrolls (Matt Drake #36)

The Alicia Myles Series
Aztec Gold (Alicia Myles #1)
Crusader's Gold (Alicia Myles #2)
Caribbean Gold (Alicia Myles #3)
Chasing Gold (Alicia Myles #4)
Galleon's Gold (Alicia Myles #5)
Hawaiian Gold (Alicia Myles #6)

The Torsten Dahl Thriller Series
Stand Your Ground (Dahl Thriller #1)

The Relic Hunters Series
The Relic Hunters (Relic Hunters #1)
The Atlantis Cipher (Relic Hunters #2)
The Amber Secret (Relic Hunters #3)
The Hostage Diamond (Relic Hunters #4)
The Rocks of Albion (Relic Hunters #5)
The Illuminati Sanctum (Relic Hunters #6)
The Illuminati Endgame (Relic Hunters #7)
The Atlantis Heist (Relic Hunters #8)
The City of a Thousand Ghosts (Relic Hunters #9)
Hierarchy of Madness (Relic Hunters #10)
The Contest (Relic Hunters #11)
The Maestro's Treasure (Relic Hunters #12)

The Joe Mason Series
The Vatican Secret (Joe Mason #1)
The Demon Code (Joe Mason #2)
The Midnight Conspiracy (Joe Mason #3)
The Babylon Plot (Joe Mason #4)
The Traitor's Gold (Joe Mason #5)
The Angel Deception (Joe Mason #6)

The Rogue Series
Rogue (Book One)

The Disavowed Series:
The Razor's Edge (Disavowed #1)
In Harm's Way (Disavowed #2)
Threat Level: Red (Disavowed #3)

The Chosen Few Series
Chosen (The Chosen Trilogy #1)
Guardians (The Chosen Trilogy #2)
Heroes (The Chosen Trilogy #3)

Short Stories
Walking with Ghosts (A short story)
A Whispering of Ghosts (A short story)

All genuine comments are very welcome at:

davidleadbeater2011@hotmail.co.uk

Twitter: @dleadbeater2011

Visit David's website for the latest news and information:
davidleadbeater.com

The Sacred Mask

CHAPTER ONE

Guy Bodie raised a mug of coffee and took a sip. The brew was hot and strong and black, just how he liked it. Bodie took his time to savour the mouthful and then turned to his dinner plate, loaded with two bacon sandwiches.

To his right, Heidi ate a chicken salad and sipped water. She smiled at him and touched his arm. Heidi's frizzy hair had been recently washed and Bodie could smell the fresh shampoo. He found it an odd contrast to the smell of fried bacon.

To his right the redhead, Cassidy Coleman, sat sipping hot coffee and staring at a croissant as if she wanted to kill it. She wasn't in the best of moods, having had a rough night's sleep, and wasn't particularly conversant. Cassidy was a physically powerful presence, always appearing to be the team's bodyguard. The truth wasn't too far from the image.

Also around the lunch table were Jemma, Yasmine, Lucie and Reilly. The full relic hunters team out for a meeting and a bite to eat. They were sitting outside at a far table with no one else around them. The New York city day was bright and warm and noisy, the nearby road full of vehicles crawling by. There was a tall black railing fence between their table and a pedestrian walkway where all manner of people came and went. Bodie saw businessmen with their black briefcases and long coats. He saw tourists with their cameras and rucksacks and hats that read 'I Heart New York'. There was a homeless man wandering and a mother and young child shopping and several youths who looked like college kids. A snapshot of New York. In the background, Bodie saw delis and upscale eateries and clothes shops and establishments that sold electronics. He watched the human traffic for a while, wondering where they were all going, what their goals were, and then he fixed on the vehicle traffic, and saw similar faces and aims there. It was a hopeful mass of humanity, and everyone was intent on something.

Bodie took a bite of the sandwich to take his mind off his surroundings and savoured the taste. He chewed for a while, looking at the others. They had recently come off a mission where they had found a lost galleon and heaps of treasure. Now it was in the authorities' hands and the relic hunters were at a bit of a loss as to what to do next.

Bodie started the conversation by nodding at Heidi. 'How far along are we with the agency thing?'

Heidi finished eating before she spoke. 'Well, we all agreed to form a new agency so that our team can earn money professionally. That was a few weeks ago. Since then, I've found out just how hard that's gonna be and how many hoops you have to jump through. It's not cheap, either.' She paused.

The team had decided to form themselves into a reputable agency and pursue the work they loved. Relic hunting. They had an excellent reputation and lots of contacts and thought they could make a good living. They were experienced and never backed down from a challenge. And they had all the right ingredients to make their team a highly capable whole. Heidi had looked into ways of forming the agency and had come up with nothing but drawbacks.

'It's gonna take longer than expected,' she said.

Jemma, who knew some of the issues she was up against, leaned forward. 'I can second that. It's a matter of working through each problem a bit at a time. Sort one, and move onto the next. We have a long list to sort through.'

'But it's doable?' Bodie asked for the benefit of the team. He, too, knew something of what they were up against.

'Given time, yes,' Heidi said. 'I need to knuckle down to work for about a week. If I don't come up for air, I might get a quarter of a way through the work.'

'Can you divide some of the workload?' Lucie asked. 'We're all here to help.'

'It's tricky. It involves US law too, so you Europeans aren't gonna be much use. Hell, *I'm* not much use. But I can get by.'

'Well, I'm here if you need me,' Lucie said, and everyone seconded her comment.

Bodie sat back, still munching the bacon sandwich. 'It's a shame we can't start advertising the agency before it's official.' He was half joking.

'It'd get some jobs in,' Cassidy replied. 'Which is what we're craving for.'

'Are you kidding?' Yasmine said. 'Reilly and I are enjoying the downtime.'

Bodie had noticed Yasmine and Reilly spending

more and more time together, and Yasmine's words were telling. Reilly squirmed a little. The pair had been a couple a long time ago, but since meeting up again after Reilly joined the team had kept their distance. Now, the opposite seemed to be happening. Bodie knew they had been out on at least one date together and were probably looking for more. Hell, he was enjoying the downtime too, able to look after his and Heidi's relationship far more easily.

'Well, I'm not,' Cassidy was a hands-on, action-orientated kind of person and didn't enjoy lounging around. Bodie could see her now. Eyes constantly peeled, looking for some kind of engagement to take part in. 'It's been weeks since our last mission, and gyms and nightclubs and male strip joints don't cut the mustard.'

Bodie smiled. Cassidy had recently taken Jemma and Lucie to their first male strip club. Bodie still wasn't sure what Jemma and Lucie had made of the experience. They didn't seem overly enamoured with the memory. Lucie had said that maybe another trip would help them make their minds up.

'I'm sure something will come up soon,' he said.

Cassidy grunted.

Bodie looked at the others. 'So, until Heidi cracks this new agency, what are we gonna do?'

Heidi finished chewing a croissant. 'It may take a while,' she said.

It was right then that Bodie's phone started to ring. He looked startled at first, but then fished it out of his pocket and looked at the screen. 'Blocked number,' he said.

'Interesting,' Cassidy said.

The Sacred Mask

Bodie answered the call. 'Hello?'

'Who's this?' a whispery, frightened voice said.

'The man you called, I hope.'

'Bodie? Is that you?'

'Yeah. Who the hell is this?' Bodie was well aware the man sounded scared and rushed.

'It's Gingham. Do you remember me?'

Bodie frowned. Gingham was a very old contact. He'd joined Bodie on a few jobs he'd pulled in London years ago, way before the relic hunters formed. That was the time of Jack Pantera. Everyone who was any good worked for Pantera, but Bodie always insisted on stealing only from those who deserved it. Never from anyone innocent. That was how Bodie lived with himself and what he did. He remembered Gingham being involved in some of those jobs, and he remembered Gingham was an excellent asset.

'I remember you,' Bodie's mind was miles away, trawling through what felt like ancient times. 'How have you been?'

'Listen Bodie, I don't have time to reminisce. I don't have much time and I'm in danger. But I have information. I've kept tabs on you. I know what you do now, and you're the only person I can bring this to.'

Bodie gripped the phone tighter. 'The only person? What's wrong, Gingham?'

'As I said, I'm in danger, so let's be quick. I know what you do now,' he repeated. 'That makes you the only man I can think of to help.'

'What do you need?' Bodie sat forward.

'I have important information. I know you save

relics. Now listen. I've been told that someone powerful and unpleasant is planning to steal the funerary mask of Tutankhamun. You know, the one in Egypt? It's gonna be one of the most spectacular heists ever.'

Bodie took a breath. The funerary mask of Tutankhamun was one of the most famous and amazing relics in existence. His mind was a temporary blur. 'What?'

Gingham repeated himself and then took a deep breath. 'You need to stop it, Bodie. A job has been sent out, the job is the mask. Someone bad is gonna do it. The cops don't believe me, not me. I'm a known criminal. It has to be someone on the inside, someone like you. Only you can stop this going down.'

'Only me?' Bodie was still trying to play catch up.

'That's right. This is big. And you're a major player in the relic game. I know. Also, to be fair, you're the only person I know in the relic game. But it has to be you, Bodie.'

'You want us to *foil* a heist? That's kinda the opposite of what you and I used to do.'

'It's the opposite of everything I've ever done, and nothing you've tried before. I'm just trying to help here. Like I said, my contacts among the cops aren't interested. Either because I'm a criminal or because old relics don't really do it for them. They have bigger fish to fry.'

'But why are you so bothered about it?' Bodie had to ask.

'I'm trying to turn over a new leaf,' Gingham said quietly. 'I'm doing better now.'

'And this helps your conscience?'

'Yeah, yeah, it does.'

Bodie understood. he'd gone through a similar experience himself many years ago. There was nothing like that feeling of trying to do better, to make amends, and fighting off the urge to take another job. It was like fighting an addiction.

'So you want me to save the funerary mask of Tutankhamun,' Bodie said softly, and everyone around the table blinked in surprise. 'What sort of information do you have?'

'Information?'

'Yeah, like who's involved, who's sent out the job, put up the money? What do you have for me?'

'Oh, I see. Well, it's all very much on the down low. Very quiet. I don't have much at all, I'm afraid. All I have is the name of the guy who blabbed about it to me. You could try to track him down.'

'What's his name?'

'Jack Ferriman. He goes to Grainger's Gym in New York. That's another reason I chose you. Because you're near to Jack.'

Bodie shook his head. 'That's it?'

'That's all I have, mate.'

'It's not much to go on, Gingham.'

The silence was like a shrug. Gingham clearly had no more to give and was anxious to get off the line. Bodie told him he'd look into it, ended the call, and then looked around at the others.

'Wanna save a magnificent old relic from getting stolen?'

CHAPTER TWO

Bodie put the phone back in his pocket and looked around the table.

'You want us to foil a heist?' Yasmine said doubtfully.

Bodie knew they'd only heard one side of the conversation and filled them in. Once he'd finished, they sat there with mixed emotions in their eyes. Bodie saw suspicion, excitement, and doubt. He saw interest, especially in Cassidy's. To be fair, he wasn't sure how he felt himself.

'Can't hurt to check into it,' Cassidy said immediately, eager.

'The funerary mask of Tutankhamun,' Lucie said, already in research mode. 'That's a big one.'

'And well guarded, I'd expect,' Reilly said. 'Which means the team stealing it will have to be exceptional.'

Bodie drank more coffee. 'What do we know about the mask?' he asked.

Lucie always had her trusty laptop with her and slipped it out of her bag and onto the table. She started tapping quickly.

Heidi prodded Bodie's arm. 'How much do you trust this guy?'

'Gingham? He was dependable back in the day.

Very dependable. We helped each other out of a few scrapes. Parted on good terms.'

'I wonder what he's been doing since you parted ways,' Heidi said meaningfully.

Bodie got her drift. 'More of the same, I guess,' he said. 'After I went, Gingham probably remained a thief. It's how he'd know about the mask.'

'But it can't hurt to whip across town and check this lead out,' Cassidy said. 'It's something to do, at least.'

Lucie was trying to get their attention with a few waves. 'All right,' she said. 'The funerary mask of Tutankhamun. It is the one I was thinking of, the one with his face. Everyone knows it, or has seen it. It's displayed in the Egyptian museum, in Cairo, and was discovered in 1925. The mask has been dated back to 1323 BCE. And, hell, it's priceless. I'm sure anyone stealing this wouldn't be able to sell it except in a very dark, private sale.'

'Some nefarious collectors want art just for themselves,' Heidi said.

'That's true, and maybe that's the case here. The mask is one of the most famous, recognisable ancient artefacts. It was carved from two layers of inlaid gold and glass, and houses precious gemstones. It depicts the face of the boy king himself.'

'Who discovered it?' Bodie asked.

'That would be the British archaeologist Howard Carter. He discovered the king's tomb in the 1920s. The mask was buried with Tutankhamun's mummy for 3000 years and bears a spell from the Book of the Dead across its shoulders. It has been called 'the best known object from Egypt itself.'

'I can see why some immoral collector would want it,' Yasmine said.

'It must be high on black market lists,' Bodie said.

'All the more reason to start this job,' Cassidy was itching to go.

'How about we just tell the police?' Heidi said.

'They wouldn't believe us,' Bodie said. 'You heard what Gingham said. He's already tried.'

'Yeah, but we're not criminals like he is,' Heidi said.

'We have no proof. No evidence. It's like 'he said, she said.' And we have no idea when it's gonna happen, or who's behind it. More evidence is required before sharing anything with the police.'

'I agree with Guy,' Reilly said. 'At the moment, we have nothing but the word of a career criminal.'

'Speaking of that,' Lucie said. 'How far would you trust this guy?'

Bodie raised an eyebrow speculatively. 'Good question. But what he did was a selfless act. He can't be gaining anything out of calling me.'

'Unless he's setting us up,' Reilly said, thinking off the rails, something he was good at.

Bodie's eyes widened. 'I can't believe that. Gingham may be a criminal, but we have a history.'

'In any case, all we're doing is going to meet a guy at a gym,' Cassidy said. 'Hardly a crime, is it?'

Bodie finished his coffee. 'She's right. We have a piece of the puzzle with Gingham. All we're doing is looking into the next piece of the puzzle. This Jack Ferriman. I can't see how it hurts to do so.'

'We're not getting paid for it,' Heidi said with a strained smile.

'It's not Gingham's fault the agency isn't set up yet,' Bodie said. 'And it sounds like we have to act now. In any case, Gingham wouldn't pay us for this, anyway. Quite the opposite, actually.'

The others still seemed reluctant. Bodie didn't want to let his old friend down. No, it wasn't the kind of thing they were used to. But it was something different – trying to *stop* a heist. It would add a string to their bow.

'If we succeed,' he said. 'It'll add new positives to our resume. We might gain new contacts. It's favourable.'

Heidi nodded along with him. 'You're right about that, at least.'

Jemma looked like she hadn't thought of that. She nodded too. 'The more advantages, the better,' she said.

Bodie felt he'd swayed them with the argument. He looked around. People swarmed about the café, thronging the sidewalk, and the road was packed with vehicles. The hustle and bustle of New York was in full flow. He saw the servers flying between tables, trying to keep up with their customers' needs. There was a busy chef in the kitchen, working furiously. And here were the relic hunters, killing time, kicking back. He felt like Cassidy for a moment – wanted to get into the thick of the action. But then he remembered what that meant – often they ended up on the front line and almost killed. Maybe it was good to take a little downtime.

No, he decided. 'We should take this job,' he said.

'It's hardly a job,' Jemma said.

'No, but it is worth our while. And it's not like we

have to travel too far,' he looked at Lucie. 'How far is this Grainger's Gym?'

Lucie tapped for a few minutes and then pursed her lips. 'It's off Broadway near West 72nd. Not far from Gray's Papaya.'

Bodie remembered a few guilty meals there. He checked his watch. 'In this traffic,' he said. 'That's half an hour. I say we go check it out. What the hell else are we gonna do with our day?'

It was mid-morning. The sun was out, and the day was warm. There was nothing else on their agenda. Bodie's words echoed around the table.

'Time to hit the gym,' Cassidy said with a grin.

The others all nodded, some of them resignedly. There really wasn't anything else to do and, since they had an interesting lead, they might as well follow it up. Bodie, in particular, wanted to do good by his old friend.

They finished their food and drinks and left the table.

CHAPTER THREE

Traffic was heavy, and it took a while for the cab to thread its way through to 72nd. Once it did, it stood in a long line of vehicles, edging forward steadily. Bodie and the others just stared out the window of the extra-large cab, watching the world go by, staring up at the buildings. Bodie wondered what was going on inside them, imagining every kind of scenario. It was forty-five minutes before they reached Grainger's gym.

They climbed out of the cab into the busy street, suddenly surrounded by noise. The gym stood adjacent to the sidewalk, a glass fronted building through which you could see a vast array of machines and the people who used them. The gym looked busy, and the people behind the glass were moving and sweating profusely.

They entered through big sliding glass doors, walking into an air-conditioned lobby. Bodie saw a small café to the right and a wide reception to the left. A single person manned the reception, and it looked pretty quiet. The guy was leaning on the till, looking bored. Bodie looked at the others.

'Jack Ferriman then,' he said.

'Any ideas?' Lucie asked.

'A few,' Bodie asked. 'I hope you're ready for more coffee.'

They trooped through to the café area and sat where they could easily view the reception. They ordered coffees and nursed them slowly. The team sat back, watching the reception, knowing they were here for the long haul.

They didn't speak much, just stayed observant. In particular, they watched the lone guy who manned the desk, observing his movements. The guy just stood there most of the time, checking in the odd customer and buzzing them through another set of glass doors into the gym proper. He took a few phone calls, always polite. As they watched, another guy came in to man the reception, and there were suddenly two people to worry about. Bodie cursed under his breath.

They watched the two guys some more and ordered another round of drinks. It was slow going.

Hours later, Bodie started to talk.

'Every hour, the blonde guy disappears for ten minutes. My guess is a smoke break. That leaves our pony-tailed guy alone.'

'We need a distraction,' Yasmine said.

'Have you clocked the filing cabinets?' Cassidy said.

'Yeah,' Bodie nodded. 'That's where all the personal information is. Ponytail has been in there a few times.'

'So how do we distract ponytail?' Heidi mused.

'I know how,' Yasmine said. 'Just leave it with me.'

They waited for the blonde to take his next smoke break. It was mid-afternoon by now and they'd all had too much to drink. Bodie thought you could only drink so much coffee and bottled water. They waited for the blonde to make his move.

It came around ten past three. He rose in the manner they'd become accustomed to and said something brief to ponytail. Then he headed away from the reception towards a set of rear doors.

Now was their window.

'Get ready.' Yasmine rose to her feet.

Bodie and Cassidy had been selected to be the searchers. The team made ready. They watched Yasmine make her way over to the ponytail and catch his attention. They could hear what was being said from where they sat.

'It looks like a nice gym,' Yasmine said, leaning on the counter.

The ponytail eyed her. 'Do you wanna join? We have all the best facilities and machines.'

'I'd like a closer look,' Yasmine said, giving him a big smile. 'Would you show me around?'

'Oh, I'm on reception. I'm not supposed to leave here.'

'But I just saw your friend leave.'

'Well, yeah, I guess so.'

Yasmine leaned in closer, eyes just a few feet away from ponytail's. 'It'd only be for a few minutes. Can't you show me around?'

Ponytail swallowed. He couldn't look away. He bit his lip and then licked both of them. Yasmine's charms were definitely affecting him. Reilly made a sound of amusement to Bodie's left.

'Go girl,' he said.

'I'd be really grateful,' Yasmine smiled again and shifted, her body language open. The ponytail stared at her.

'Two minutes?'

'That's all it'll take, I promise.'

The ponytail looked around, saw no other customers around and made a fast decision. He nodded at Yasmine and then came around the reception. He had a keycard in his hand and used it to open the doors into the main gym. The sound of grunting and machines and music filtered out.

Bodie and Cassidy rose swiftly to their feet. The reception area was empty. They crossed the space and entered reception as if they belonged there. Bodie went immediately to the filing cabinet and Cassidy hung by the front of the desk in case she was needed to ward anyone away. To the others, they looked like normal workers whiling their day away.

Bodie examined the cabinet. The first drawer was labelled A-E, the second F-K. Quickly, he slid open the second drawer and took hold of the manila file that held all the Fs. He flicked through them and came to the one labelled Jack Ferriman. Bodie opened it and took in the information it contained.

It wasn't in-depth, but it held a photo ID and a home address. Bodie memorised the picture and the address. He looked over at Cassidy. A smiling customer was approaching her.

'Hey,' a short blonde woman said. 'What do I have to do to join this place?'

Cassidy tapped the desk in front of her. 'One hundred press ups,' she said. 'One hundred crunches. And then we'll see what you can do with the plank.'

The woman blinked, and then her face fell. Her mouth opened in a big O. 'Wh...what?'

Cassidy gave her a wide smile. 'Just kidding. If you wait here a few moments for my colleague to return, he'll be able to help you.'

'Th...thanks.'

Bodie left the counter area, Cassidy at his side. 'Well done,' he whispered.

'Did you get the address?'

'Got it.'

They rejoined the others and then made a sharp exit from the gym. Outside, they waited for Yasmine. Soon, she had rejoined them and the team was ready to move. They didn't want to discuss things in front of a cab driver, so made their way to a café first and took seats at the back. They ordered drinks all round.

'Now we have an address for Jack Ferriman,' Bodie said after a few sips. 'But we can't just get dropped off outside his apartment and wait around in the street. What's the plan?'

'We're gonna have to hang around and wait for the guy,' Cassidy said. 'Chances are he won't be in when we call around.'

'He might be,' Reilly said.

'We don't get that kind of luck,' Jemma said. 'I thought you'd know that by now.'

Reilly grinned. 'Your luck changed when I joined up.'

Lucie just stared at him. 'Ya think? Treks through the Amazon, kidnapped to take part in a deadly contest, a deep sea treasure being hunted by your old gang. Need I go on?'

Reilly clammed up and took a huge gulp of coffee.

Bodie leaned forward. 'There's only one option.'

'Yeah,' Yasmine said. 'We hire a car and sit our asses in it until he turns up.'

'I feel like a detective,' Bodie said. 'Isn't that what they do?'

'Sit outside properties and wait for its owner to turn up?' Cassidy said. 'I don't think so.'

'But we are detecting,' Bodie said. 'Another string to our bow.'

'Don't jump too far ahead,' Heidi said. 'We don't even have a car yet.'

Bodie finished his drink and sat back. He watched Lucie take her phone from her pocket and start looking up hire car companies. She needed somewhere close, and quick, and she wasted no time Googling the options. Soon, she was speaking to someone who promised them a hire car within the hour.

'Done,' she said.

'So, it's a visit to Ferriman's,' Bodie said. 'And a little chat. We'll find out where he got the information about the mask.'

'We'd better do it quick,' Lucie said. 'We don't know when the heist is going down.'

Bodie rose to his feet. 'You're right. Let's go.'

CHAPTER FOUR

It was getting dark outside by the time the team had collected their car.

Bodie drove. Ferriman lived in Hell's Kitchen, so Bodie found himself following 9th Avenue most of the way until he reached West 47th Street. Here he turned off, following a narrow street with cars parked to both sides and three-storey houses with basements and steps running up to their front doors. He drove a while longer, turning twice, and eventually found himself on a wider street where he could get a parking space and sit watching the front steps that led up to Ferriman's building. Nobody had spoken for a while, probably because they were all cramped inside the large size SUV.

'Do you remember what he looks like?' Cassidy asked with half a smile on her face.

'I bloody well hope so,' Bodie replied, peering intently. The area at the top of the steps before the porch that led into the building was illuminated and would help spot Ferriman.

The team waited. It was gone 7 p.m. At 7.15 a young family came out, all wearing coats and hats. They zipped and shuffled and tugged for a while and then headed purposefully down the steps, perhaps going out to dinner. At 7.35, a tall man with a bald head sauntered out the door and then down the steps, taking his time. He wore a heavy backpack and looked like he was going on a long trip. More time passed. The team tried not to get restless. At 8.05, an elegant lady wearing a shiny dress appeared and waited for a cab to turn up.

'Non stop action,' Reilly commented.

People entered the building too. None of them was Ferriman. The team waited. 8.30 came and went and then 9.00. Bodie realised he hadn't eaten in a while and started to get hungry. Lucie moaned she was starving.

'We're not really cut out for this surveillance lark, are we?' Jemma said.

Bodie admitted it was weighing on him, too. 'I don't see what else we can do?'

Right then, a figure exited the building and stood in the light. Bodie could see him clearly. 'That's Ferriman,' he said.

They all grabbed for the door handles but Bodie told them to wait. They needed to see his intentions first. Ferriman descended the steps at pace and then climbed quickly into a parked car. They wouldn't have had a chance to get close. Ferriman started the car up and then drove off. Bodie followed.

They cut down one road after another, getting stuck in traffic. Bodie stayed a few cars back, but he didn't think Ferriman would check for surveillance. It was crazy New York traffic; it was dark, and it was a man going about his daily business. Bodie wondered just who Jack Ferriman was and how he fitted into the puzzle.

After half an hour but having not travelled too far,

Ferriman cut right into the cramped parking lot of a small pub. Bodie turned in after him, grabbing the last available space. Ferriman wasted no time locking his doors and hurrying inside. The team watched him go, sitting in darkness.

'We gonna accost him in the pub?' Cassidy asked hopefully.

'Too public,' Bodie said. 'We need to get him alone.'

'Then we wait for him to come out,' Heidi said, looking around. The parking lot was badly lit, lots of shadows cast around the parked cars. When Ferriman came out, they could easily approach him for a word.

They waited again, trying to get comfortable. The pub was busy, people coming and going all the time. In the time they waited, they saw all manner of things going on – petty drug deals, a man and a woman slipping into a nearby alley, two men flailing in a drunken fist fight. They passed the time in silence, everyone waiting for Ferriman to make an appearance.

At 10.36, he did. He walked out of the door alone, looked around, and then buttoned up his coat. He started across the lot towards his car.

Bodie and the others climbed out quickly and let him get into deeper shadow. As the man approached his car, they stepped forward, an intimidating group.

'Jack Ferriman?' Bodie said.

The man, a tall, short-haired forty-something with a face that looked like it had been carved in several places, narrowed his eyes. 'What of it?' he asked suspiciously.

'If you're Jack Ferriman, we need to ask you some questions,' Heidi said.

'I'm not Ferriman,' the man tried to push past them.

Bodie grabbed his right shoulder and gently eased him back. 'Not so fast, mate. I know you're Ferriman, and I need to ask you a couple of questions.'

'Piss off.' Again, Ferriman tried to squeeze past them.

Bodie got in his way. 'You're not going anywhere 'til we get some answers.'

Ferriman glared at them, taking in the team that faced him and, probably, their resolve. He swallowed, then glowered. He looked back toward the pub as if seeking help, but there was nobody else around. Bodie stood in the dark and watched him.

'Ask your questions,' Ferriman finally said.

'Recently,' Bodie said. 'You've been shooting your mouth off about the theft of a sacred artefact. Tutankhamun's funerary mask. You've heard something, and we want to know what it is.'

Ferriman's eyes narrowed to mere slits. He took a breath. 'Someone told you I blabbed?'

'You got it,' Cassidy said.

'I don't know anything about some funerary mask. I don't even know what that is.'

Bodie wondered how to handle it. He hadn't expected Ferriman to be too cooperative, but had been hoping for the best. He stepped forward, pushed Ferriman against the nearest car, and frisked him. Satisfied the man wasn't armed, he turned him around and took hold of his collar.

'We don't have time for bullshit. Now tell us what

we want to know or I'm gonna set Cassidy here on you and the outcome isn't gonna be pretty.'

Ferriman glanced at the redhead. 'I think I'd like a bit of that.'

Cassidy didn't hesitate. She stepped in and punched Ferriman in the gut, then brought an elbow down onto the man's exposed neck. Ferriman grunted and fell to his knees, head down. Bodie hauled him up.

'You need to learn manners,' he said.

Ferriman didn't have time to blink before Cassidy hit him again, this time a blow to the solar plexus. Ferriman's face twisted in pain and he shuddered, grabbing Bodie's shoulders to keep from falling. The rest of the team crowded closer to shield the activity from prying eyes, but there was no one around to see. A dull thudding noise approximating music came through the door and windows of the pub.

Bodie let Ferriman's hands rest on him. Ferriman's hands were curled into fists and he looked like he wanted to fight. Bodie gave him a humourless smile. 'You wanna tangle with her? Your funeral.' He stepped away.

Ferriman shuddered on the spot. He was a man caught in about a dozen minds. He looked from Bodie to Cassidy and then back again.

'But I don't know anything about no funerary mask.'

Bodie nodded at Cassidy. The redhead raised her fists again. This time, Ferriman flinched. He lowered his head and raised an arm. 'No,' he said. 'Don't.'

'Then tell us what we want to know. Tell us, and we'll be out of your life forever.'

Ferriman looked torn, as if telling would physically hurt him. He screwed up his face. 'Who ratted on me?'

'I will not tell you that.'

'Why not? They're just a rat.'

'So are you, but here we are...talking. Now tell me what you know or this is gonna get a lot worse.'

Cassidy threatened him again with her fists.

'All right, all right,' Ferriman threw his arms up in the air. 'Like I said, I don't know anything about no *funerary* mask. All I know is what someone told me. They were merry, you know? They'd had a few. The guy said that one of the world's biggest heists was about to go down. Some mask in Cairo that's real famous. Belong to Tutankhamun. It's a big deal, apparently. This guy was real gushy about it. Anyway, he said someone was planning to steal it, and that's all I know.'

'Who's planning to steal it?' Bodie asked.

'I don't know. He didn't say and I know better than to ask.'

Now Heidi got in Ferriman's face. 'Who was doing the talking?'

'Eh?'

'Who told you the mask was going to be stolen?'

Now Ferriman looked scared. 'Oh shit, I can't tell you that.'

Cassidy unleashed another punch that drove Ferriman to the ground. Bodie left him in a groaning heap for almost a minute before hauling him up. Now, he put a hand on Ferriman's throat and squeezed.

'Give us a name,' he said.

Cassidy hovered in the background, staying close.

Ferriman looked like he was about to throw up. He could barely stand. Bodie's hand around his throat might have been the only thing keeping him upright.

'Damn,' he said. 'Can you just stop hitting me? I haven't done anything wrong. It's just information, that's all.'

'Give us a name,' Bodie repeated.

Ferriman looked trapped. His eyes were wide and filled with pain. Finally, as Cassidy stretched once more, he nodded. 'Wait, wait,' he said. 'There's a guy called Winter. They call him that because he's a cold-hearted bastard. Winter runs with a gang called the Old Boys in New York. They have a bad rep; they're ruthless. And there are more of 'em than you.'

Bodie nodded and let go of Ferriman's throat. They stepped away then and watched him get in his car and drive away.

'I think that went really well,' he said.

CHAPTER FIVE

They returned the SUV and found a late-night restaurant. They ordered food and sat around as they waited for it to turn up, sipping drinks. Bodie was enjoying a cold bottle of beer. There was an accomplished air around the table.

'Well, we know it's all real,' Lucie said. 'Now we've heard the same info from three different people.'

'It's gonna get tougher though,' Reilly said. 'We're talking about a gang now.'

'I like tough,' Cassidy said. 'It's my middle name.'

'It's still not enough to turn over to the authorities,' Bodie said. 'It's all hearsay. They probably get a dozen threats a week.'

'And yet the criminal underworld seems aware of it,' Heidi said. 'It's like Chinese whispers out there.'

Their food arrived, and the team tucked in. Bodie had ordered steak and took his time cutting it into pieces before starting. The conversation died for a while, and then Lucie said, 'We're at a crossroads. What the hell do we do next?'

'I guess we gotta track down this Winter character,' Cassidy said.

Bodie nodded and swallowed some steak. 'All we know is that he belongs to a gang.'

'He sounds notorious,' Heidi said. 'I think someone will be able to find him.'

'Who do we know in New York?' Reilly asked.

They had various contacts across the world. People they'd worked with; people they'd helped. New York was one place they'd operated in more than once.

'Jake Scholes,' Bodie said. 'NYPD. He helped us out a couple of times, if you remember?'

They did, all nodding. Bodie checked through his phone and brought up Scholes' number. 'It's maybe a bit late to call him now,' he said.

'I'll call him,' Cassidy said with a smile. 'It'll make his day.'

Bodie grinned. He remembered Scholes had been sweet on Cassidy. Something about her red hair. He checked the time again.

'I guess it's not too late after all.'

They finished up their meal and then ordered some more drinks. Cassidy fished her phone out of her pocket and called Scholes' number. The police detective answered on the first ring.

'Yeah? Who the hell is this?'

He didn't sound happy, maybe because of the timing. Cassidy put on her best silky voice.

'Hey, Jake, this is Cassidy Coleman. Remember me?'

'Ah, yes, hey.' Scholes' voice changed. 'How could I forget?'

Cassidy spent a few minutes chatting before getting to the point.

'We need your help, Jake.'

'We? Oh, so you're all in on this? I was hoping it was a more personal call.'

Cassidy smiled. 'I bet you were. Those are the breaks, Jake.'

'Maybe if I help you out we could go get a drink sometime?'

Cassidy's smile deepened. 'Maybe we could.'

There was a brief silence, and then Scholes spoke again. 'What do you need?'

'We're looking for someone. The guy's a gang member and he's called Winter.'

'All right. I don't get involved in that side of things, but I know a man who does. Give me a few.'

Cassidy thanked him and hung up. Bodie grinned at her. 'Looks like you got a date.'

'He's a nice man. Could be a lot worse. And, in any case, a girl's gotta keep feeding.'

They killed some time in the restaurant, staying until closing time. They were hoping Scholes would ring back tonight. Eventually, though, there was nothing to do but return to their homes and see the night through. When morning dawned, Bodie was already awake, staring at a curtained window and wondering if Scholes had called Cassidy back. He checked his phone for the tenth time. Nothing. He rolled over and looked at Heidi. Still asleep. The whole scenario around the mask was troubling. It shouldn't bother him so much, but he felt deeply concerned about it. It felt like destiny. The once-thieves had been tasked with saving an ancient artefact from being stolen. It all felt right to Bodie.

And so he was on edge.

So far, all roads led to a guy named Winter. This Winter was part of a gang. It could be dangerous, so they'd be better off isolating the man. See what he knew. If they could isolate him, they could intimidate him into talking. He wondered briefly when the mask was due to be stolen.

Bodie checked the time. He got up, grabbed his phone and went off to make bacon and eggs and coffee. Heidi would appreciate it. Bodie pottered around in their little kitchen for a while, constantly checking his phone. When breakfast was ready, he gently woke Heidi, and the couple sat in the front room, taking their time. By now the sun was up, streaming in through the window, and it looked like it was going to be a nice day.

'I guess Jake Scholes doesn't love Cassidy as much as we thought he did,' Heidi said, now eating toast.

At that moment, the phone rang. It was Cassidy. 'We have to meet,' she said.

She rang them all. They met at a café on Broadway. They drank coffee and tea and listened to what Cassidy had to say.

'Listen. Jake Scholes came through.' She blinked and smiled. 'And now I have to take him out for a meal,' then she shrugged. 'But he's a nice guy, so I can deal. Anyway, his contact told him that Winter is a gang member of the Old Boys. They're over in Harlem and have a few places of business, but the main one is a nightclub, a famous one called The Black Bourbon Rooms. It's hard to get in, apparently. But Winter is there every night. Scholes even sent a snapshot through to my phone.' She shared it around, showing them what Winter looked like.

'Any info on these Old Boys?' Bodie asked. 'What do they do?'

'It's all vague. But they're into drugs, gambling, prostitution. All the usual sins. They're not known to be especially violent, but they look after their turf, don't let anyone muscle in on them. They're well run by a gun named Meeks, apparently. He's been the head honcho for a decade.'

'And where does Winter fit into this gang?' Reilly asked.

Cassidy shrugged. 'He's a lieutenant. That's all I know.'

'He may even have guards then,' Reilly said.

'We need to find him first,' Heidi said.

'In the middle of a popular nightclub?' Lucie asked. 'With everyone around? The noise, the music, the dancing. And then we're gonna get in his face and ask him what he knows about the theft of the funerary mask?'

Bodie nodded with raised eyebrows. 'That's the idea.'

'We'll find a way to isolate him. Don't worry,' Cassidy said. 'That's what we do.'

'No. Finding ancient relics is what we do,' Lucie said. 'This is different.'

'It's important we stop this theft,' Bodie said. 'We're invested in it now. We can't let it happen.'

'Unless we steal it ourselves,' Jemma said with a smile to show she was joking.

'Don't go there,' Bodie said.

Cassidy sat back and crossed her legs. She sipped her tea. 'Then I guess we're going clubbing tonight,' she said. 'Any excuse to get dressed up.'

She looked at Jemma and Lucie. 'You ready, girls?'

The day passed slowly for Bodie. He wasn't looking forward to the prospect of visiting the club just to interrogate a lead. There was also the problem of how to isolate the man. Maybe they could follow him out and approach him then.

The night came around and Bodie and Heidi got dressed. They looked ready to party, ready to hit the west end hard, as Bodie said, a throwback to his days in London. The team got taxis to the Black Bourbon Rooms and met up outside. The club wasn't open yet and there was already a line. Bodie and his team joined the end of it.

The night was cool and noisy. There were hundreds of twenty and thirty somethings gathered together in the semi-dark, waiting for their turn to face the doormen and then walk through the doors. Bodie shivered. He wasn't dressed for the cooler weather. None of the others looked happy either, apart from Cassidy.

'I think we're passed our nightclub days,' Bodie said. He could hardly hear his voice above the surrounding hubbub. People pushed and pulled each other and shouted in each other's faces to all sides. Music poured out onto the pavement. Some people were dancing in the street.

'Speak for yourself,' Cassidy said. 'This is my heaven.'

Even Jemma and Lucie looked unhappy. 'It's cold,' Lucie said, stamping her feet to keep warm.

'We'll get there,' Bodie said hopefully.

The line shuffled along slowly until Bodie and the others reached the doors. They were given the once over by the doormen and then ushered inside. Bodie found himself in a long corridor surrounded by flashing lights and hordes of people. They all moved forward slowly, heading towards a larger space ahead with more flashing lights. Bodie reached it first, the place opening out into a wide, noisy, thumping club. They were on a mezzanine with a handrail, and able to look into the pit below where hundreds crowded a dancefloor, gyrating in all directions. There was a stage which the best were plucked from the crowd and pulled onto and, to the left, a long glistening bar area, again crowded. To the far right were mini-stages where professional dancers did their thing. Ahead, Bodie saw private booths with red plush seating, some with curtains drawn. He looked from left to right and thought about the enormity of their task.

'Finding him in here's going to be a nightmare,' Bodie said. 'So let's get started.'

They split up, made sure their phones were on vibrate so they'd feel any messages going to the group chat, and started sifting through the crowd. Bodie made his way down to the first floor and started looking, using a grid formation in his mind. The dancefloor wasn't difficult, the people not really moving from the spot. The stage was easy enough, too. Then he headed for the bar.

Throughout the club, the team ranged. They crossed each other's paths, checking as they went. With seven of them, it was easier than expected to get a full scan of the nightclub in a little under an hour.

Bodie hadn't quite finished looking. He was now studying the private area, the booths beyond several corded ropes. There were no guards to keep people out so, if he couldn't quite make out a face he wandered among them, scanning carefully. The private booths were filled with well-dressed men and women, most of them glittering with gold, all sipping their champagne and their beer that was balanced on glass and mosaic tables. The music was quieter back here, the atmosphere less frenetic.

Bodie studied face after face, the impression of the man called Winter burned into his brain. Finally, over ninety minutes since he started looking, Bodie saw the man.

Winter was reclining in the furthest booth, his large right arm draped around a woman's shoulders. To his left, three men sat, all wearing suits and not looking especially happy. Bodie stared at Winter for a moment.

'That's our man.'

CHAPTER SIX

The team crowded around. They didn't stare at Winter, but the guy was on their radar. The three men sitting with him looked bored and were staring at everyone who passed. They were probably bodyguards. Their eyes lingered on the relic hunters.

'We can't get close,' Heidi said.

'You know we can,' Cassidy said with a smile. 'Just look at us.'

'He has a woman, and he looks pretty into her,' Lucie said. Winter was now kissing the woman beside him.

'He hasn't met me yet,' Cassidy raised an eyebrow.

Bodie turned firmly away from Winter. 'Do we wait, or do we go ahead? That's the question.'

'It'll be easier in a crowded club,' Reilly said. 'Less chance of a battle than confronting him out there in the street or a parking lot.'

Bodie wasn't so sure, but the team unanimously decided that they should confront Winter right here and now. He respected that. Carefully, he checked out Winter's position. Although the man sat in a booth, there was nothing stopping an approach.

Only the three alert bodyguards.

Winter was distracted. Bodie wondered if one of the bodyguards might get up to visit a restroom, easing their options. He decided to wait a while. The team melted away to watch from afar. The music thudded and bodies gyrated around them. Dry ice filled the air for a while. People shouted at each other, leaning their heads close. Bodie watched and waited.

Some time passed. The bodyguards didn't move. Cassidy had brought them soft drinks to sip, to help blend in, and now Bodie finished his off.

'No more waiting,' he said.

The team was ready. Together they approached Winter's booth. The bodyguards clocked them straight away, their eyes narrowing. Bodie didn't slow or veer away. He just headed arrow straight towards Winter.

They were twenty feet away, then fifteen, then ten. The bodyguards rose to their feet to intercept them. Bodie made a fast dash at the last second, and beat them to Winter.

He leaned down to tap the man's shoulder. Winter was currently sucking face and jerked involuntarily. His eyes went wide, his face shocked, as he clapped eyes on Bodie. He blinked. The woman beside him looked shocked, too.

'What the fu-' he started to say.

'I need to talk to you,' Bodie said. 'Ask you a question or two.'

'Are you kidding?' Winter was now trying to see around Bodie, clearly wondering where his bodyguards were. 'Get away from me.'

At that moment Bodie felt a hand fall on his left shoulder. He turned to see one of the bodyguards standing right next to him.

'You need to leave,' the bodyguard said with an American accent.

'I don't want to,' Bodie returned.

His team was now crowding the bodyguards. Nobody spoke, and nobody moved, but tension laced the air. Winter was staring as if he couldn't believe what was happening. Bodie leaned in to him.

'I just need a moment of your time, pal.'

Winter looked at his bodyguards. 'Get rid of them.'

One of the men narrowed his eyes. 'In here?'

'What do I pay you for? Get rid of these assholes.'

Bodie felt the hand on his shoulder tighten. All around them, the nightclub pounded and rocked to the sounds of music and laughter. The man tried to force Bodie away, but Bodie stood his ground.

'Get off me,' he said.

It was escalating. Cassidy was in one man's face, Heidi another. The bodyguards were trying to push the team away. Cassidy and Heidi were backed up by Reilly and Yasmine, and the team didn't budge.

Winter was watching closely. The woman at his side didn't seem too concerned and began to stroke his thigh. Winter suddenly looked distracted as the woman's hands moved back and forth. He turned to her, away from Bodie.

'Maybe later, babe.'

'Normally, you like it.'

'Yeah, but I'm a little preoccupied right now.'

The woman didn't stop. Winter turned back to his bodyguards. 'Seriously? Is that all you can do?'

Bodie braced himself. The bodyguards were working themselves up to a fight. They still seemed concerned by their surroundings, but they would listen ultimately to their boss. The man holding Bodie's shoulder took his hand away.

And brought it swiftly back in a balled fist.

The punch connected with Bodie's stomach, made him fold. Bodie gasped. Lucie was at his back. She struck out, caught the bodyguard a glancing blow across the cheek whilst he recovered. The bodyguard stepped back.

Cassidy blocked a fist, sent it harmlessly past her right cheek. She stepped in and kneed her opponent in the groin. He twisted at the last second, negating the blow. He skipped away, slammed into a table, and staggered. Cassidy was on him in an instant.

Heidi traded blows with her opponent, the pair slamming each other around the head. Nobody gave an inch.

Those people close by were starting to see the commotion and stopping to stare. Once upon a time there might have been screaming or raised voices – today everyone just took out their phones and started filming.

Bodie dodged a kick from the bodyguard facing him. He grabbed hold of the leg and twisted. The man gasped and collapsed to the floor. Bodie could have leaned in to finish him off right then, but, instead, he bent towards Winter.

'One simple question,' he said. 'Then we're gone. Your bodyguards can't stop us.'

Winter suddenly looked anxious. He stared at the skirmish. Cassidy was standing on her opponent's ribcage, threatening his neck. He writhed under her, his face a mask of fear.

Heidi elbowed her man in the right eye, making him cry out in pain. His hands flew up to his face, leaving his lower parts completely unprotected. Heidi made space to kick him in the stomach and then followed up with a slam to the back of the head. The man fell to his knees before her.

Bodie took a chance. He left his opponent lying on the floor and reached out to grab Winter. The man's eyes grew large. Even the woman beside him pulled away.

'The funerary mask of Tutankhamun. How do you know it's going to be stolen, and what else do you know?'

Winter froze, his eyes narrowing. He shook his head. 'What?'

Bodie repeated himself more slowly.

'The mask? The sacred mask? That's all you want?'

Bodie nodded. Winter laughed. Whilst he laughed, his bodyguards took more blows to their tender parts and staggered back and forth. He didn't seem to notice.

Bodie leaned in further. 'Tell me.'

Winter stared at the plethora of phones pointed at them and all the people standing around. The music and the dancing and all the conversations continued as if nothing was happening.

'I don't know what you're talking about.'

Now Bodie turned all his attention to Winter. He leaned over the man and punched him in the gut. He grabbed hold of his chin and twisted.

'The next one will break your nose.'

'Men!' Winter yelled.

But they were beset. They most assuredly weren't holding their own. They were on their backs, bruised and struggling.

Bodie squeezed Winter's jaw harder. 'Tell me what you know.'

Winter struggled. It was then that the woman beside him launched herself at Bodie. She was silent and fast and hard, flinging her fists at his face.

Bodie defended and fell back. He let go of Winter. The woman attacked more fiercely. Bodie grabbed her wrists and twisted her around so that she faced Winter. He gave her a push in the spine, sent her tumbling. She fell over the glass and mosaic table, landing headfirst on the floor.

Bodie punched Winter in the face. The man squealed. He shouted for his men again, oblivious to their plight.

'The mask,' Bodie said.

Winter threw up his hands. 'All right, all right. Back off. What the hell do you want to know?'

CHAPTER SEVEN

'I already told you,' Bodie said. 'The mask. How do you know someone's planning to steal it and who will it be?'

'I can't believe that's all you want. It's such a small thing. I don't know anything, not really.' Winter was holding his chin where Bodie had bruised it. 'You've gone to a lot of trouble for nothing.'

'Then there's no reason not to tell me.'

Winter looked over at his struggling bodyguards. 'Let them up.'

Bodie shouted to his friends, asked them to stop fighting. The team stood back, relented. The bodyguards struggled to their knees, shaking their heads. There wasn't a lot of blood, but there were plenty of bruises.

Bodie wondered if Winter was playing for time. Maybe he had more men coming. Maybe he would set the same men on them again. Anything was possible.

Cassidy and the others left the bodyguards to it, and crowded around. Now everyone stared at Winter. To his left, the woman who'd attacked Bodie climbed back into her seat, looking sulky.

'I'm not sure how I feel about this,' Winter said finally. 'I feel like I've been forced into revealing some information, but it's info I don't really care about. It's the method that annoys me.'

'I gave you a chance to make it easy,' Bodie told him.

'Hey, fuck you, man. Don't you know who I am?'

Bodie spread his hands. 'We're here, aren't we?'

'What the hell is that supposed to mean?'

'We tracked you down. Clearly we know who you are.'

Winter took that on board for a second, then glanced at his bodyguards. 'I guess I'm gonna need some new guys.'

'Don't blame them,' Cassidy said. 'We're very good.'

'Can we get to the point?' Reilly asked. 'I want to get out of here.'

Bodie saw that, whilst most of the watchers had wandered off when the action ended, some were still hanging around, looking on. Maybe they were hoping for more. Nobody appeared to have reported the commotion.

Winter shuffled in his seat. 'All right,' he said. 'The funerary mask of Tutankhamun. Yeah, there are whispers everywhere. Someone's planning to pilfer it. Nothing concrete. Nothing certain. It's more like rumours, rumours that are half in the air, if you know what I mean. That's been going on for a while.'

When Winter took a breath, Bodie said, 'Go on.'

'I found out through a fence I use to smuggle European artefacts. The guy's never wrong. You can count on his word. He told me in passing over the phone not so long ago.'

'What's his name and where does he live?' Bodie asked.

Winter again looked shifty, but then sighed. 'All right. His name's Germaine. He lives in Paris. He's over there now.'

Bodie looked at the rest of his crew. 'Paris?'

'Yeah, you know, the one in France.'

'What else do you know?'

'That's it, man. Germaine is very private, as you can understand. All I have is a phone number and an email address.'

Bodie grabbed both and then, tentatively, left the nightclub with his team. They had wrested as much information out of Winter as they were going to get. Once outside, he turned to the others.

'We have a big decision to make,' he said.

CHAPTER EIGHT

The team immediately retired to a quiet all-night diner off Broadway. They'd visited it before and knew, after midnight, it quieted down considerably. Once there, they ordered drinks and snacks and sat back in the large, plush red booths.

'This thing is expanding considerably,' Bodie explained. 'It's not so hard when you're chasing down leads in your own backyard. But Paris-'

'The one in France,' Heidi interrupted.

'Yeah, that one. I mean, Paris? That's a whole new thing. We're gonna have to be seriously committed to go to Paris and chase some guy down named Germaine.'

'If we can even do that,' Reilly said.

Bodie paused whilst their drinks were served. He took a great gulp of hot coffee and then sat back. 'How committed to this thing are we?' he asked.

'Can we contact the authorities and hand it off to them?' Yasmine asked.

'I don't think so,' Heidi said. 'We don't have enough for them. So far, it's all just hearsay and, as we said before, they probably get dozens of threats per week.'

'We're not being paid for this,' Cassidy pointed out.

'And we don't have our new agency up and running yet,' Bodie said. 'We're not getting paid for anything.'

Heidi nodded. 'Good point. We're months off getting the agency up and running.'

The team sat for a while, pondering the choice. It was Lucie who broke the silence. 'I, for one, respect and love all ancient artefacts. I can't imagine something as important as the mask of Tutankhamun disappearing forever. I couldn't forgive myself if I let that happen.'

Bodie had also fallen in love with ancient artefacts during the last several years. He was already feeling guilty about not advancing further. He nodded at her. 'It's a good and fair point. I feel a responsibility now when it comes to artefacts. We've discovered and saved enough.'

Jemma nodded her head. 'I feel it too.'

Reilly hadn't been on the team long. 'I'm beginning to know how you feel,' he said. 'But I'm easy either way.'

Lucie said, 'We can't simply let it go. We've come this far. We can't just give up. If, in two or three days, something happens, we'll know that we failed. And that will be harder.'

'Harder than what?' Cassidy asked.

'Going to Paris.'

Bodie looked at the others, received nods of agreement. None of them had any objections regarding Paris, and most of them were keen on it. He sipped more coffee and then waited as the snacks were served. He ate a few chips from a big red basket before continuing.

'We can't just go blindly,' he said. 'We need a lead.'

He made a phone call. Jack Pantera answered on the third ring.

'Hey, mate, how's everything going?' Bodie asked.

'As well as can be,' Pantera said. 'It's been a while.'

Jack Pantera was Bodie's old boss when he used to be a thief, mostly in London. Pantera taught him and directed him and helped him. Pantera aided Bodie to steal only from those who deserved it, mostly criminals. It was a risky trade, but they managed to keep it going for years.

'You still under surveillance?' Bodie asked.

The phones were probably tapped. But the watchers, the CIA, knew that Bodie knew they were there. They'd been watching Pantera for years, even taking care of him.

'The usual,' Pantera said.

'I need your help. The team do.' Bodie went on to explain everything that had happened so far and why he needed to find a guy out of Paris by the name of Germaine. Pantera listened carefully.

'You still have contacts in Paris?' Bodie asked, finally.

'Sure. I have contacts all over Europe.'

'Do you think you can make a few calls? Maybe ferret out this Germaine?'

'Any idea who he works for?'

Bodie shook his head despite being on the phone. 'Not a clue. All we know is he's a fence who handles European artefacts. And he's probably good because he has wide-ranging contacts.'

'All right,' Pantera sounded dubious. 'You're

gonna have to leave it with me. I'll call you back.'

Bodie ended the call. He knew he'd given Pantera a tough task, but the man was very good at what he did. There was nobody better to ask and, if Germaine was top flight and operated out of Paris, someone would have heard of him.

'Now we wait,' he told the others.

It was late, so they parted and went home. Bodie left the phone on loud all night, but Pantera didn't ring back. The next morning they met up again at a local café and the others looked at Bodie expectantly.

'No joy,' he said. 'Pantera could be struggling.'

Coffee appeared, and then the phone rang. Bodie looked at the screen. 'It's him,' he said, and placed the device in the middle of the table before putting it on speakerphone. They had the eatery to themselves. 'We're all here,' he said.

'Good. Damn it, Bodie, you know how to make me work. I've been up all night, answering and fielding phone calls. Paris is five hours ahead of New York. You know how hard it is to get criminals out of bed in the early hours of the morning?'

'I thought that was when they did their best work,' Reilly said.

'That's the people who work for them. I'm talking about the people at the top. They keep regular hours.'

'Thanks for doing this, Jack,' Bodie said, a little lamely.

'You're welcome, mate. Don't worry about me. I'm just grumpy from lack of sleep. Anyway, I found your man. A fence named Germain does work in Paris, central Paris, but he has a few local haunts near the Bastille. I can send you a picture. And he's not just a fence. He's a drug dealer, too. You're gonna have to be careful with this one.'

Bodie made a face. 'I hate drug dealers.'

'Yeah, don't we all? Apparently, this Germaine is near the top of the tree, well-respected, and has several people working for him. I don't know about offices or a HQ, but I can give you a few places to search. Bodie, I have to say, it's a tentative lead.'

Bodie knew it. 'The team's invested in this, Jack,' he said. 'We can't walk away and then see, a week later, the relic being snatched. We can't do that.'

'So you're going to Paris?'

Bodie looked at his team, studying their faces. There was positivity in every expression and several nods of the head. He knew they were up for it.

'We're going to Paris,' he said. 'Wish us luck.'

'Wait. There's something else.'

Bodie had been about to sign off, but now leaned forward. 'What is it?'

'During my enquiries, I asked discreetly about Tut's mask. There're no whispers, no chatter, among my contacts. That's strange. My associates tend to know everything that's going on.'

'The whispers seem to be passing along a grapevine,' Bodie said. 'An exclusive grapevine. Only a few people are involved. That's why we need your help.'

'There was one rumour though,' Pantera went on. 'An old rumour. It went like this. A while back, a guy called the Salamander was interesting in acquiring this mask.'

'Who's the Salamander?' Heidi asked.

'Not much is known about the Salamander,'

Pantera said. 'He's a big time crook operating throughout Europe. He enjoys ancient artefacts and is rumoured to possess quite a few that he shouldn't, but it's never been proven. It's all hearsay. For a crook, he's very solitary and hard to find.'

'But he was interested in Tut's mask?' Bodie asked.

'That's the story. He even tried to buy it from the Egyptians. That's pure arrogance. The guy clearly lives in a different world to normal people. Obviously, the Egyptians sent him packing. Now, maybe, he's organising this heist.'

'Maybe,' Bodie said. 'Could you look into the Salamander for us?'

Pantera grunted. 'He's a very dangerous guy. One of the worst. I wouldn't want my name associated with his in any way. Until you're sure, let's stay well enough alone.'

Bodie acquiesced. He thanked Pantera for the information and then sent the photograph of Germaine to the group chat so everyone could get a look. The team sat back with their drinks and looked at each other.

'It feels like a turning point,' Heidi said. 'Like we're really throwing ourselves into this.'

Bodie nodded. 'The more we discover, the more invested I am. Now we have this Salamander in the mix. But Germaine is the big target, and the next stop is Paris.' He drank up. 'Shall we?'

CHAPTER NINE

By the time they landed in Paris, it was eleven o'clock that night. The team went immediately to a hotel and settled in. They would begin their search for Germaine the next day. Despite the long hours of travel and the time difference, Bodie wasn't tired and spent most of the night staring at the ceiling. Heidi could sleep anywhere, anytime, and was snoring softly beside him. He watched her a little, still marvelling that they were together. A couple. It had been a long time coming and now that it was here, he was determined to make the most of it. He wouldn't drive her away as he had others in his life. Bodie valued his friends the most, and Heidi had become one of the best, the closest. Their relationship was still relatively fresh and new, and that was good, but it was definitely leading somewhere, and that was better. He hoped she felt the same way he did. By all accounts, she did.

They woke and breakfasted the next morning and then decided to hire a large car. What they needed to do couldn't be accomplished using taxis or Ubers. By the time they'd hired a vehicle, the morning was gone. It was mid-afternoon when they started to drive around Germaine's haunts. They took their time, staring out of the windows and hoping for a glimpse.

'I wonder how accurate these locations are,' Yasmine said, looking at buildings and down side streets.

'The intersection of Dorian and Picpus,' Bodie said. 'Jaucourt and Picpus. The Place de la Nation. And three clubs we can check out later. My guess is that's where we'll find him.'

They cruised the streets, hoping to catch a break but, hours later, they were no further forward. Bodie found a place to eat, and they spent some time there as they waited for the clubs to open. Evening fell, the streets darkening and then becoming golden with street lighting.

Bodie drove to the first club on their list and found a place to park so they could see the front door. Of course, if Germaine chose to enter through the rear or sides, they were screwed. With that in mind, he sent Cassidy and Heidi to watch all the other doors, to surreptitiously watch from the shadows, and plugged in their comms system. They had brought it from New York for just this sort of eventuality.

They waited, hoping to get lucky. It didn't happen. Germaine didn't show. After a few hours Bodie moved to the second location, hoping for a glimpse. Again, nothing materialised. They all had Germaine's picture, kept in close, but the man was a no show.

As the evening grew older, Bodie drove them to the third location. This one was shabbier than the others, and quieter. There was no queue outside, and only one bouncer on the doors. Bodie easily found a place to park and hunched down, watching the comings and goings.

About 23.30, Germaine showed up.

He came around a far corner, hunched up against the chilly night air, with three of his cronies. Bodie could see them easily under the stark light of a streetlamp. They were pooled in its glare. They stood for a moment, smoking vapes, the smoke whirling around in great mushroom clouds.

'Shall we?' Cassidy said quietly.

'We need him alone,' Bodie said. 'These are dangerous men.'

The four men stood and talked for a while, and then Germaine stopped as he was approached by someone. Bodie distinctly saw him hand over a small plastic packet to the man and pocket some money. Germaine's friends took no notice, but Germaine didn't part from them for long. Soon, he was back in their company, chatting. Bodie thought he saw weapons thrust into the men's waistbands, maybe guns, maybe knives, something bulky. Five minutes later, Germaine was approached by another man and repeated his process. Ten minutes after that, a couple came up to him. Germaine sold them the dope.

'Quite a business he's got going on here,' Lucie said.

'We could nab him now,' Yasmine said. 'There's only four of them.'

'This is different,' Bodie said. 'We're in a strange country facing dangerous criminals. Drug dealers. The best idea would be to nab Germaine when he's alone.'

'I wonder if he keeps to a routine,' Reilly said. 'So we know when and where he'll be. His buyers seem to know he'll be there at this time. And the bouncer's taking no notice.'

Germaine was only a dozen steps from the front door of the club, doing business, but no one seemed to mind. He appeared supremely confident. Bodie lost count of the number of transactions he saw, the men always staying together. It became obvious that the other men were bodyguards.

An hour later, Bodie saw Germaine break away from the group. He walked some way down a narrow alley and then shuffled up to a wall. He was mostly in darkness. Bodie realised the man was relieving himself against the wall.

'He's all alone,' Cassidy said. 'And the alley has two entrances.'

Bodie nodded. 'It's a possibility.'

'You wanna nab him whilst he's taking a piss?' Reilly said with surprise in his voice.

'If it's the only time he's alone...' Bodie let the sentence hang.

They watched Germaine for the rest of the night and then followed him out of the area. They worked in groups of twos and threes, in front of and behind the drug dealers. The relic hunters were skilled in stealth, in keeping quiet, in remaining unobserved. It was part of their old job. A big part. Bodie enjoyed re-using some of those skills now.

Germaine paced to another building and stood outside for a while, selling his little packets of death. The night passed. The team watched. Not once was Germaine seen on his own. His men conversed and stamped their feet against the cold and smoked their vapes continuously. They watched each sale carefully, keeping Germaine safe.

It was a long night. It ended on a bad note when they followed Germaine back to his apartment and saw all four men going up together. Even here, at the place he lived, he was not alone. The team gave a collective sigh.

'Could it be any harder?' Reilly said.

'We're back to the alley,' Cassidy said, as if relishing the prospect. 'It's the only time he's alone.'

'We could pick him up again tomorrow,' Lucie said. 'Follow him again. Maybe things will change.'

'I don't want to waste too much time,' Bodie said anxiously. 'If we do this another night, it's another night lost.'

'So it's the alley,' Cassidy said. 'We catch him whilst he's draining it.'

'Using sudden brute force,' Reilly said. 'As we know, these guys are dangerous. They won't hesitate to kill us.'

'We take Germaine and interrogate him,' Bodie said. 'Drag him away from the area. Take our time. When we're done, he doesn't know who we are, he hasn't heard our names. Then we dump him and make our getaway.'

'Tomorrow night then,' Yasmine said. 'It's gonna be fun waiting in the alley.'

Bodie shrugged. 'It's what we have to do. I mean, look how far we've come. Yesterday, we had no idea who Germaine was. Now, we've identified a way to question him. And we can utilise our old skills whilst we're doing it. We get to be sneaky, crafty and furtive. I like the sound of that.'

Cassidy was grinning, thinking back to the old days. 'Me too. I love using the old skills.'

'I don't have any old skills,' Lucie said. 'What will I do?'

'Stay at the back,' Bodie said. 'This job is for the thieves.'

CHAPTER TEN

The next evening was as cold as an arctic blast. The team made their way to the dark back alley an hour before Germaine was due to arrive and took their places. Cassidy and Bodie crept closest to the spot they expected Germaine to visit and hid behind two metal bins they dragged into place. The others hung back in the shadows, ready to act. Bodie and Cassidy hunkered down to wait.

Bodie had never found the waiting difficult. If you were waiting for a mark to leave the house, to enter an establishment, to go to bed, or to take a piss, it was all the same. It was a collection of clear and precise moments that inevitably passed by. Seconds ticking. His mind focused, ready for what was to come.

Beside him, Cassidy was the same, out of the same school. They were the best at what they did. And Cassidy was even more lethal than he was.

The others waited, ready to act. Lucie had been left back at the car, making a quick getaway easier.

Bodie crouched and waited. The night crawled around them. The sounds of the city filtered up and down the alley – the roars of engines, the thudding of tyres, the chatter of passers-by, the sound of distant thudding music. As he watched, Bodie occasionally saw Germaine and his cronies passing across the mouth of the alley. It was good to know the man had turned up.

An hour passed. Bodie hoped Germaine would feel the call of nature. He needn't have worried. As if on cue, the man came sauntering down the alley, shoulders hunched. He approached Bodie and Cassidy's hiding place, stopping just before it. Bodie stayed absolutely still, feeling Cassidy tense at his side. They waited for Germaine to take his place. Bodie took a last look around Germaine, making sure his pals weren't following, but why would they? They knew what was happening.

Germaine grunted and then unzipped. He leaned against the wall. This was the time. Bodie and Cassidy shot up. Bodie approached on stealthy legs, Cassidy a step behind. They came up to Germaine, and he didn't hear them. Bodie looped an arm around Germaine's throat and Cassidy slipped around his front, holding a hand to his lips.

'You speak, you die,' Cassidy whispered. 'Nod if you understand.'

Germaine's eyes were wild, and he didn't struggle. After a moment, he nodded, and then tried to zip himself up. Cassidy shook her head.

'He's more worried about putting the little pink thing away than his own neck,' she said. 'If you don't cooperate, you lose it. Understand?'

Cassidy presented a knife and held it up before Germaine's wide eyes. The man nodded very quickly.

Bodie manhandled him down the alley, towards the rest of the team. They moved quickly but carefully, making no noise. Germaine was shivering, and not just from the cold. He walked on rubbery legs, stepping with difficulty. Bodie propelled him forward, keeping him upright. The others joined them and led the way to the car.

Lucie was waiting for them at the far end of the alley, the car parked at the kerb. The team ran and threw open the doors. Bodie and Cassidy bundled Germaine into the back seat. Bodie still had his arm around the man's throat.

Doors slammed. Lucie started the car up and drove away. Germaine was theirs. Bodie loosened his arm a little. Cassidy nestled her knife in his ribs just enough so that he could feel the tip.

'We have a few questions for you,' Bodie said in an even voice. 'If we don't like them, you get the blade. Understand?'

Germaine nodded, his eyes still wild. He was breathing heavily, shuddering. He seemed to have some kind of tic in his right eye. Bodie kept his arm around the man's throat, loose enough to let him speak.

'The funerary mask of Tutankhamun,' Bodie said. 'You know it's going to be stolen and have blabbed about it. *How* do you know?'

Germaine swallowed heavily. He looked confused. 'The mask?' he repeated in a thick voice. 'You want to know about the mask?'

Cassidy jabbed him a little with her knife. 'You heard the question. Now answer it.'

'But I'm just a dealer of old relics,' Germaine said. 'I hear all sorts of things and talk to many people. I hear so much, I don't remember it all.'

'Stop trying to be cute,' Cassidy said, pressing the knife in even further.

Germaine gasped and tried to wriggle away. In response, Bodie tightened his grip around the man's throat for a few seconds. 'There's nobody here to protect you, Germaine,' he said. 'Your ours. We can do anything we like to you.'

'And believe me,' Heidi said, turning around. 'Drug dealing scum like you should be locked away for life.'

'I don't make them use it,' Germaine protested. 'I just sell it. The users are the scum.'

Bodie stared at him incredulously. The man's words had thrown him off track. He shook his head, trying to get them out of his mind. He didn't want the conversation veering off in that direction.

'Stop lying and playing for time,' Cassidy said. 'I will cut you.'

Germaine winced, tears at the corners of his eyes. 'I believe you. But I just can't remember anything about the mask. I'm sorry.'

Bodie thought the man was tougher than he appeared to be. Here he was, almost crying, but still holding out. He could tell by the man's ragged breathing that he was terrified.

'I think we're gonna have to cut him,' Bodie said.

Germaine's breathing got much worse. His body shook. He watched as Cassidy pulled the blade from his ribs and touched the tip against the top of his leg.

'This is gonna hurt,' she said.

Bodie covered Germaine's mouth.

Cassidy pressed the knife into Germaine's leg. First his trousers cut, then blood welled up through the tear. The knife went in slowly and inexorably. Cassidy applied even pressure so that it went steadily. Germaine could watch himself gradually and deliberately being stabbed. He squirmed. He tried to yell, but Bodie had him in a grip of steel.

'We have all night,' Bodie whispered in his ear.

Germaine was yelling against Bodie's hand. His muscles were straining. Veins stood out at the side of his neck, all corded. Cassidy pressed the knife in for a full minute, but it didn't go in that far. After that, she relented, drawing it out and watching Germaine's leg bleed.

'That was a taster,' she said. 'It'll get much harder after this.'

Germaine tried to take a huge breath. Drake inched his hand away from the man's mouth to let him. 'Don't scream,' he said threateningly.

They let Germaine calm down for a while. The blood soaked through his trousers. Cassidy still held the knife dangerously close.

'Same question,' Bodie said after a while. 'The mask.'

'You would do this to me all night? You are evil.'

Again Bodie was taken aback. That the drug dealer could be so sure that *he* was in the right and they were wrong. A psychologist would have a field day with this man.

'Evil begets evil,' Heidi said and left it at that.

Cassidy rested the tip of the knife against Germaine's leg and looked at him questioningly. 'What will it be?'

'I can't help you.'

This time she didn't dally. She jammed the knife into his leg hard, letting it travel to the halfway point. Then she pulled it out and jammed it in again. Bodie could barely keep hold of the bucking drug dealer.

'I'll perforate you like a goddamned cullender,' Cassidy said.

And she sank the blade in again; three cuts now. Germaine was crying and gasping and trying to stop her with his hands.

'Move your hands,' Cassidy said. 'Or your fingers will get chopped off.'

'Stick him again,' Bodie said for show. 'Don't stop until he talks.'

Cassidy raised the blade.

Germaine held up both hands, suddenly gasping more loudly. He waved his hands wildly. Bodie took his own hand away from the man's mouth.

'You got something to say?'

'This is big. Very big,' Germaine said. 'Please don't tell them where you got the information. They are terrible, and I would never go against them. They would make me pay way worse than you.'

'What the hell are you talking about?' Bodie asked.

'The Rossi gang. They're from Italy. I got the information from their top guy, a man named Nico Rossi. It was just a casual conversation, nothing major. Rossi dropped it in just out of the blue.'

'If you're lying to us, we'll be back,' Cassidy threatened. 'You saw how easy it was to snag you this time. Don't invite us back by giving us a lie.'

Germaine was constantly gasping in pain and crying and blabbering. He waved his hands. 'I'm not lying. Please. I'm telling you the truth.'

Bodie told Lucie to stop the car, and they rolled Germaine out into the street a few miles from his favourite haunts. That's how long it took to break him. Bodie sat back and turned to Cassidy.

'Well done.'

'I hate drug dealers.'

'What about gang leaders?'

'Them too.'

'Then let's go to Italy.'

CHAPTER ELEVEN

Italy was much warmer than France when they landed the next day. Bodie had taken the time to call Pantera and ask him to come up with some information regarding the Rossi gang. He was still waiting for a reply.

The team made their way to their hotel and hired a car from the lobby. It was a big, black seven seater beast with sliding doors and it stood out a little too much. Still, there was little they could do. It was all the hotel could offer on short notice. By the time they were ready to make a move, Pantera still hadn't called back.

With nothing to do, the team took some down time and did their own thing. They didn't stray far, expecting the call at any minute. It was mid-afternoon by the time it came.

'What do you have for us?' Bodie asked immediately.

'Steady on, mate. This took an arm and a leg, not to mention two fingers.'

'Funny. Sorry, Jack, we're kind of on a deadline here.'

'Yeah, I get that. Listen, the Rossi gang is bad news. They run a rough part of Rome and they're killers. They're tight too, and well-manned. I have a few addresses for you. One stands out above all the others. Nico Rossi is the top dog, right?'

'Yeah, so I understand.'

'Well, he owns a gun club in south Rome. It's in the Portuense area. Nico Rossi has people all over that area and farther south. I don't know how you're gonna get near him.'

'Does he hang out at the gun club?'

'You might be able to pick him up there. Listen, I'll send you pics and details. Sorry I can't be more use.'

It was thin, Bodie thought, but it was something at least. They knew where the gang operated. They had an address for at least one establishment. They knew Nico Rossi was actively involved. All they had to do was get close.

To a gang boss? Easier said than done.

Bodie contacted the others and called everyone together. They sat in the hotel lobby and discussed Pantera's information, trying to decide what to do.

'We investigate,' Reilly said. 'We go to the gun club and start asking questions.'

'That's just an easy way to get yourself killed,' Cassidy warned. 'We need to be more subtle.'

They made their way to the right area and found the gun club. It was a wide, squat concrete building that reflected the sun's light. It had a faded yellow sign outside that said *Maximo's*. Ironically, the sign was peppered with bullet holes.

Bodie found a place to park. The team split up, ignored the gun shop, and made their way to several close establishments.

Bodie chose a bakery. When he walked in, Heidi at his side, it wasn't busy. He went straight up to the counter. 'Hi, do you speak English?'

The frizzy-haired woman looked confused, but the tall man wearing a white apron standing behind her turned and smiled. 'I do,' he said. 'A little.'

'It's about the gun club,' Bodie said. 'Maximo's. We're looking to talk to the boss. A man named Nico Rossi. Any ideas what times he keeps?'

If you didn't ask, you didn't find out.

The team spent the rest of the day questioning the locals, those who spoke English, and trying to find out even a little snippet of information concerning the gun club. They watched it closely too. An hour after they arrived, a car full of men in suits turned up, disgorged its passengers and drove away. The suits adjusted their sunglasses, looked around and turned towards the club. Nobody talked. After a minute, they all went inside. Apart from that activity was quiet. Bodie saw only two patrons enter the club, both of them carrying bags.

The team met in their car and drove out of sight of the gun club so they wouldn't attract attention.

'Learn anything?' Bodie asked.

'Yeah, everyone's scared of the damn place,' Heidi said. 'There are hoods going in and out every day of the week. More hoods than customers.'

'From what I can gather, it's a staging area,' Reilly said. 'An important one. I think it could be a major hub of Nico Rossi's business. We need to get eyes on the back.'

'We can't do surveillance on the place,' Jemma said. 'These are professional criminals. They'd spot us in the first hour.'

'And we can't pretend to be interested in joining the club,' Bodie said. 'It's not like we're locals or even speak the lingo.'

'Maybe we could rent an apartment above a shop,' Reilly suggested. 'I noticed one of them was free.'

Bodie considered it. 'Maybe. But it still doesn't bring us closer to Nico Rossi. We don't even know if and when he's in there. How do we get closer?'

Even as he sat there, Bodie saw another carload of men in suits driving past. The men's sunglasses flashed as they went by, and all heads turned towards the team's car.

'We should get out of here,' he said. 'We're too conspicuous.'

They drove away from the place, back towards their hotel. There were no tails, no men in suits following them. By the time they reached the hotel, the entire team was miserable. They sat in the car for a while, talking.

'I have an idea,' Cassidy said after a while. 'There's absolutely no reason we shouldn't visit the gun club. It's still in a touristy area. It's on a main road. We just have to look and act like tourists. See it from the inside. Act a bit dumb and excited.'

Bodie nodded. 'It's a step forward,' he said. 'Maybe we'll catch a break.'

'Maybe Nico Rossi will be serving behind the counter,' Reilly said sarcastically. 'That'd be a break.'

'Do you have a better idea?' Cassidy asked.

Reilly bit his lip. 'Not really.'

Bodie thought about it. A look behind the doors of the gun club was workable. Yeah, they'd look out of place but they could act the part of tourists whilst they were getting the lay of the land. All those hoods had to go somewhere. Maybe a look behind the scenes would open up new ideas.

'All right,' he said. 'We go in, act as tourists, take a look around. But we're gonna have to be careful. There'll be more armed dudes in there than an army barracks.'

'All of us?' Lucie asked. 'Is that wise?'

'The more eyes, the better,' Bodie said. 'Everyone's good at what they do here.'

Cassidy checked the time. 'When we gonna do it?'

'We've no time to waste,' Bodie said. 'The mask is vulnerable. The thieves could strike at any time. We should go back there right away.'

They decided it wasn't too late to return to the gun club. A tourist was almost as likely to visit in the early evening as in the afternoon. They did a double check and found out that the club was actually listed as a place to visit on a local tourist page. Bodie smiled when he saw the listing.

'That works,' he said.

'Be ready for anything,' Cassidy said.

CHAPTER TWELVE

They parked up outside the club, leaving the car as close to the door as they could. They reasoned it couldn't hurt, and they might even need a quick getaway. The street was well lit, the night pressing in on the outskirts. The gun club had several lights illuminating its entrance, but two were out. The place looked shabby and unkempt.

Bodie glanced at his team one more time, nodded, and then led the way to the front door. He opened it and stepped inside the gun club. The first thing he saw was a large reception room with seating, tables, and a counter at the far end. There was a small bar to the left. Bodie saw three men in the seating area, all with mugs and plates before them. He waited for the others to enter. All eyes turned to them.

They headed for the counter. A youth with short hair and a black polo shirt that bore the name *Maximo's* stood there, his eyes calculating. When Bodie arrived, the youth said, 'I'm guessing you're English?'

'Close enough,' Bodie said.

'You want to use the ranges?'

Bodie nodded, looking every which way. So far, there was no sign of anything untoward going on, no hoods, no men in suits and sunglasses. It was just an ordinary gun club.

'You brought your own weapons?'

Bodie faked a laugh. 'We're tourists, mate. Can't bring 'em into your country.'

The youth nodded, then started ringing items into his till. He came up with a total, which Bodie paid, and then came out from behind the counter.

'Follow me,' he said.

The youth headed to an enormous set of double doors and pushed through. He held the door open for Bodie and the others. Bodie followed and found himself in a large room. To the right were more armchairs and tables where people lounged. Spread across the room in a long row were a series of gun ranges. In front of them, at varying distances, stood all kinds of targets. As he watched, Bodie could see and hear people shooting.

So far, so normal.

The team crowded inside, staying together. The youth pointed towards a series of shelves along the back wall.

'Choose whatever you want. You have an hour. Do you need me to show you how to use the targets?'

Bodie nodded, wanting to appear as touristy as possible. It was when he started walking towards the ranges that he looked to his left.

And saw something interesting. There was a large glass room up there, built on a mezzanine. It had glass walls and floor and even a ceiling up by the rafters. It perched ungainly, as if it was someone's dream that didn't really fit the surroundings. Bodie could see everything that was going on inside.

It was well furnished, with a lot of plush black leather chairs. There was a wide oak desk at one end. The desk was populated by one man, and the chairs were filled with the sunglass-wearing goons. Everything was clear. The goons lounged around, some with legs crossed, some reading magazines, others scrolling through their phones. The man sitting on the desk had a tumbler of alcohol in his left hand.

This man was Nico Rossi.

Bodie recognised him instantly. He made sure to catch everyone else's eyes and nodded to the room.

'You guys okay?' the youth asked, noticing something had passed between them.

'Great room up there to hang out in,' Jemma said. 'Can we relax up there too?'

'Oh, no, sorry. That's just for the boss. Don't go near those stairs.'

The youth continued to show them how to use the targets and then left them to it. Bodie and the others chose their weapons and went to the ranges, just for show. Whilst they were choosing, they had a few minutes to stand together out of earshot of the other patrons.

'You see Nico?' Bodie said.

'Yeah, and eight guards,' Cassidy said. 'They'll all be packing.'

'We won't get another chance like this,' Bodie went on. 'It has to be now.'

'Do you have a plan?' Lucie asked.

Bodie sighed. 'Not yet.'

'Maybe I do.' Jemma was looking at the people lounging on the chairs close by. 'See that guy's lighter, sitting on the table? We need to get it.'

'What for?' Reilly asked.

'Take one guess.'

Jemma took Reilly's hand and the two of them started walking between the tables as if heading for a corner booth. Jemma was one of the best at sleight of hand. Bodie and the others turned away, not wanting to draw attention. Jemma let Reilly get between the lighter and its owner and then reached down to pocket it. The lift took about a second and then they were walking again, soon reaching the booth.

Jemma looked towards the toilets to her right, said something to Reilly and then headed in that direction. Reilly sat at the booth, looking nonchalant. Bodie leaned over his range, trying to sight his gun. The others copied.

It was a waiting game now. The tension wracked up a notch. Bodie tried to keep the anxiety down, but, when he fired, he was nowhere near the centre of the target. What was going to happen? He was used to edgy situations, but there were a lot of hoods up in that office and they were all armed.

He sighted down his weapon again. Jemma soon came out of the toilet, her expression calm. Bodie watched her from the corner of his eye. She caught his gaze and nodded. It would all happen quickly now.

The team continued firing. They were all tense and ready to act. Bodie threw a quick glance up at the glass room. Nothing had changed.

Minutes passed. Bodie saw nothing suspicious, heard nothing out of the ordinary. He reloaded his weapon and then fired again. His shots were filling the target. Maybe he should change it. He was distracted. He aimed again.

At that moment, because he had half an eye on it, he saw smoke beginning to plume out of the ladies' bathroom. It was very slight at first, just a soft billow, and it caught no attention. Slowly, the billow turned into a cloud and it began to spread. It crept through the large hall. Someone would notice it soon.

Bodie concentrated on his shooting. He fired another round. The smoke grew worse. Just then, one of the seated men jumped to his feet and started yelling. Everyone else looked around. Someone raced off to grab the youth. People rose and stared at the surging smoke, unsure what to do. By now Bodie could no longer see the toilet door and the smoke was spreading into the room and up to the ceiling.

The youth barged through the doors. He took one look at the smoke and then ran towards it. He stopped, looked at a wall, and saw the fire extinguisher perched there. The youth grabbed it and ran for the toilet.

Bodie and the others were watching proceedings along with everyone else. There seemed little danger. Bodie looked up at the glass room. Nobody had noticed the smoke yet. It all seemed very relaxed up there.

Except then it wasn't. Nico must have noticed the smoke billowing up to the ceiling, for he suddenly pointed and started shouting. Men rose from their chairs, jumping to their feet as if electrocuted.

The youth flung open the toilet door. Smoke abruptly flooded out and Bodie could see flames. The flames spread rapidly, climbing the walls. The youth aimed the fire extinguisher at the blaze and turned it on. Nothing happened. Bodie guessed it was a dud. He yelled at the kid.

'Get out of there.'

The youth backed away. The flames were spreading rapidly. They leaked out of the toilet and caught a pile of paper targets that were stacked in a corner. The whole thing was spreading far faster than Bodie could have imagined. People were backing away now, looking to run. The entire room was filling up with smoke and the sound of a crackling fire created panic.

The glass room door was flung open. Hoods in suits ran for it. There was no ceremony, everyone pushing at once. They got stuck to start off with, but then started racing down the steps one at a time. Nico was about halfway in the pack, pushing and elbowing along with everyone else.

Bodie and his team positioned themselves near the bottom of the stairs. The hoods were rushing, panicked, barely looking where they were going. The first of them reached the bottom of the stairs and started towards the waiting relic hunters.

Bodie was in position, standing just ahead of the team, who had formed a kind of gauntlet for the hoods to run through. The hoods weren't paying much attention, just running and pushing as hard as they could. They were straggling now too, as the faster ones pushed ahead.

The first passed Bodie, eyes staring at the plumes of smoke. He let the man pass, let him run through the gauntlet. Another man ran past, then a third. Soon, there were five of them running through the gauntlet and the relic hunters struck.

They hit all at the same time, lashing out. Cassidy kicked a man in the groin. Jemma backhanded a man in the throat. Heidi smashed a nose with an elbow. Bodie tripped his man up and watched him crumple to the ground. That way, they took out five men at once, and then fell on them quickly. Bodie smashed his man's head into the ground and took away his weapon. Smoke now plumed all around them. They were grey shapes fighting in the half dark. The relic hunters sought to debilitate and removed weapons from holsters and waistbands.

Three more hoods still ran down the stairs along with their boss, Nico Rossi. Yasmine and Reilly were ready for them.

Bodie looked to the others. He saw Lucie was struggling and scrambled over to help, knocking her opponent unconscious. Cassidy knelt on her adversary's spine as she choked him into oblivion. She already had his gun. Heidi continued to smash her man's face until the lights went out in his eyes. None of them had a chance to reach for their weapons.

Nico Rossi came barrelling across the floor. Three men were with him. Yasmine tripped one, Reilly another. Rossi slowed and stared, wondering what was happening. The other man reached for a gun.

Reilly flung himself at the man, hitting him around the waist. The two of them crashed to the floor, the weapon flying away. Reilly punched the man as hard as he could in vulnerable areas whilst the situation and the smoke still confused him. From the beginning, this had been a surprise attack. It was all shock and awe.

Bodie watched as Cassidy and Heidi ran to help Reilly and Yasmine. He coughed. The smoke was getting thicker, surrounding them. The flames were crackling and growing. Bodie could feel the heat. The fire was spreading through heaps of paper targets and other flammable materials, and it was catching hold with a roar.

Bodie grabbed hold of Nico Rossi. The crime boss swung out, trying to bat Bodie's arms away or catch him across the face. He looked completely confused. His eyes flicked to his downed men with incredulity.

'What are you doing?' he managed. 'Don't you know who I am?'

Bodie patted the crime boss down for weapons, finding nothing. Then he grabbed a flailing wrist and twisted it. Rossi yelled out in pain.

'Say the wrong thing and I'll break it,' Bodie said. 'Then we'll try the other one.'

'You will all die for this.'

'Maybe, but first I want some information. Do you remember talking about the funerary mask of Tutankhamun? You told someone it was going to be stolen. I need to know where you got the information.'

Rossi was staring at him. His eyes were wide and cold and hard. He struggled in Bodie's grip.

'Fuck you. I don't know anything about any mask.'

Bodie had no time for antics. He broke Rossi's wrist and grabbed the other. Rossi squealed and almost fell to his knees. 'Second chance,' Bodie said. 'After this, I'm going for your eyes.'

Rossi was drooling with pain. He tried to cradle his broken wrist, but Bodie wouldn't let him. He was aware of Cassidy and the others standing over the fallen guards, watching them carefully.

'We haven't killed anyone,' Bodie said. 'We took your guards out with skill and ease. We could do it anytime. Now, answer the question and we'll be gone from your life forever.'

Rossi struggled. He had gone white. Smoke swirled between them. Bodie couldn't help but cough. The air was getting warm, and the fires were crackling. The acrid stench seared the back of his throat.

Bodie twisted Rossi's wrist in warning. Rossi grunted in pain.

'Last chance.'

'I don't know of any fucking mask-'

Bodie was having none of it. He broke Rossi's other wrist and then struck him in the left eye. Rossi screamed. His hands flopped. He couldn't use them to cover his eyes. He tried to hunch away from Bodie.

'No, please, don't.'

Bodie struck out again, knuckles connecting with Rossi's eyeball. The man choked in pain.

'I'm gonna take out both your eyes,' Bodie growled.

'No, no, listen. All right, all right. I heard about the mask. Tutankhamun's. But it was just a passing comment. Nothing serious. Now look what you've done to me.'

'Tell me how you know it's going to be stolen.'

'All right. It came from the Big Rat.'

Bodie shook his head. 'Big Rat?'

'It's a mole. A rat deeply embedded in another gang. The Big Rat told me he'd overheard one of the gang members talking about the mask. Thought it was good information.'

'What's the gang member's name? Who and where are they?' Bodie asked.

'His name is Garpo. He's embedded in the Chechnyan mafia in Prague. Very well embedded. He sends us all kinds of information we can act on. The mask thing is a very small part.'

Bodie threatened the man's eyes again. 'What's the name of this gang and where do they hang out?'

Rossi told him. They were called the Skaya and covered most of central Prague. Apparently, they were a notorious gang. Bodie took in all the information, holding Rossi at arm's length. The man looked exhausted. He was slumped and red-eyed and coughing. Bodie had almost forgotten about the swirling, acrid smoke.

Now reality came rushing back. The club was ablaze. People were rushing for the exit. They would make excellent cover for a getaway. Bodie shouted at the others, told them to get the hell out, then punched Rossi full in the face, sending him to his knees. Rossi hung there, head down, bleeding.

'No more,' he said.

Bodie ran for the exit. The smoke enveloped them, and he could hear the sound of crackling flames. The youth was at the exit now, looking to see if everyone had made it out. When he saw Rossi and his bodyguards, his eyes widened and he started to rush inside.

Bodie grabbed him. 'Don't bother with them. They're scum. Save yourself, mate.'

The youth wavered, then turned and ran ahead of

Bodie. The entire team was out by now. Bodie was the last one. He rushed through the door into the area beyond and then saw the doors that led to the street. Someone had propped them open. People were squeezing through, taking it in an orderly fashion now that the immediate threat was far behind them.

Bodie took his turn filing into the street. He found his team waiting for him. Together, they walked away from the smoke-filled club, blending into the street.

Cassidy was at his side. 'You get the info?'

Bodie nodded. 'Next stop Prague.'

'A gang?'

'The Chechnyan mafia.'

The team made a collective wince. 'Not gonna be easy to get close to,' Heidi said.

'We may have to change our tactics,' Bodie said. 'Let's get there first. Find them.'

The team headed into the day.

CHAPTER THIRTEEN

The relic hunters knew they had to do this right. The Chechens were no small matter. They went to their hotel, met in the lobby after an hour of eating and showering, and sat close together. Bodie plucked out his phone and called Pantera.

'What do you know about the Skaya Chechnyan mafia in Prague, mate?'

'Are you kidding? How lucky. I know everything about them.'

Bodie blinked. 'You do?'

'No! Of course not. Prague's a long way from Miami, mate.'

Bodie realised he was asking a little much. 'Do you have any contacts who might know more about them?'

Pantera sighed. 'Yeah, you know I have people in Europe. Anything specific?'

'Base of operations. Contacts. A man named Garpo, though that's a long shot. People we can approach, that kind of thing.'

'Leave it with me,' Pantera hung up.

Bodie looked at the others, still holding the phone. 'I think we're starting to get on his nerves.'

'Even Pantera has his limits,' Jemma said.

'I guess so.'

They sat around and planned their next steps. They could wait for Pantera to call, or they could start their journey towards Prague. The latter seemed the best option. They waited for Lucie to book their flights, then returned to their rooms and packed. It didn't take long. Soon, they were checking out and in a large Uber, heading for the airport. By the time they checked in and headed through security, Pantera still hadn't called.

Their flight was in ninety minutes.

Bodie checked his phone again. 'I wonder-'

It rang, startling him. Pantera's name flashed up on the screen. Bodie jabbed the button.

'Hi Jack.'

Pantera spoke for about five minutes. Nobody had heard of Garpo. He could finesse the team a meeting with some important members of the gang if need be, and he gave Bodie a few addresses. It was all good information.

'These gang members,' Bodie said. 'Are we likely to get anywhere with them?'

He could almost hear Pantera shrug. 'They're solid. Known to take a deal so long as it doesn't hurt the gang. They'll help you get close to Garpo.'

Bodie thanked Pantera and hung up, then turned to the rest of his team. 'We have info on two men who might be able to get us close to Garpo. The problem is...'

'How do we get close to the gang?' Yasmine finished.

'Exactly. We don't want to be too pushy, but we have to get close to Garpo, and fast. That's the next problem.'

Pantera had told him the Skaya were widespread, influential and feared. They didn't take prisoners, and were notorious with the police. For every member the cops put away another two popped up on the street. They were ruthless, and into just about anything from theft to murder.

'Time to rack your brains, people. We can get a meeting with these two contacts but we still have to get close to Garpo. And he's with the gang. He doesn't sound very high-up either.'

'Not a bad thing,' Reilly said. 'That means he'll have no guards.'

Bodie nodded. 'We just have to get close.'

Their flight was called. They made their way to the gate and waited to board. Soon, they were on the flight and winging their way towards Prague.

Bodie just hoped they would be in time.

CHAPTER FOURTEEN

The plane landed, and they were soon through security. They had their bags with them. They rented a car and drove it to their hotel, wasting no time. Soon, they had got rid of their bags and were back in the car, feeding an address into the sat nav.

'All right,' Bodie said. 'Let's do a little recon.'

The team spent the rest of that day staking out the two addresses that Pantera had given them. It wasn't hard work, they just had to be careful. One of the big issues was – they didn't know what Garpo looked like. He could be right in front of them and they'd never know. The first address was a fish restaurant where tough-looking men and women came and went, constantly walking in and out of the front doors in plain sight. The clientele didn't seem to notice the comings and goings, and the restaurant did a thriving trade. Bodie saw the same face only twice. The gang had many members. He could tell that most of the men and women carried guns and three times he saw the glint of steel, too. The faces entering and leaving all looked relaxed, as if they had no fears about using the restaurant as a front.

'We should set up a meeting with one of these guys Pantera mentioned,' Heidi said into the silence inside the car.

'And then what?' Bodie said. 'We need something more this time. This gang is huge. I feel like we need to be on the inside.'

The second address was a market with a building at the centre that acted as a HQ. They perused the market for a while, buying goods so they could carry bags and blend in better. Again, they saw mass comings and goings, dozens of people bringing information and carrying out orders. And this was only *two* of the gang's bases.

When they were done, they left the area and headed back to their hotel. They all met later in the bar for a conversation and a drink, sitting around a large round table in the corner. It was dimly lit and relatively quiet and Bodie could hear everyone speak. He sat back with a bourbon in one hand.

'The recce went well,' he said. 'What do we think?'

'They're organised, plentiful, and dangerous,' Heidi said. 'Exactly what we feared. We don't even know what Garpo looks like. It feels kinda like a dead end.'

Bodie wouldn't accept that. 'We can't give up now. We're too far in and the mask is still at stake. There's only one way to go as far as I can see.'

'Which is?' Reilly asked.

'We're gonna have to infiltrate the gang. Get close. Develop a little trust in a short time and ask who Garpo is.'

'Infiltrate?' Heidi repeated. 'And who the hell is gonna do that?'

'Pantera's contacts can get us in,' Bodie went on. 'We present as top class thieves, something like that. When we're in, we find Garpo.'

'You think they'll let us in that easily?' Reilly asked doubtfully.

'Not into the inner circle,' Bodie said. 'But as outsiders, yes. They'll always be on the lookout for new talent.'

'Maybe,' Cassidy said. 'But which one of us is going to do it?'

Bodie took a sip of his drink. 'Who's gone undercover before?'

The team frowned and then looked at each other. The first answer was obvious – Yasmine – the second not so much.

But Heidi eventually said. 'Me. When I was with the CIA, I often did undercover work.'

Bodie held out the flat of his hand. 'I give you Heidi and Yasmine. Our undercover specialists.'

'You think we can infiltrate the gang?' Yasmine asked. She looked doubtful.

'Of course you can, with a little help from Pantera's contacts. They'll get you in. And then you can come up with an excuse to find Garpo.'

'Risky,' Cassidy said. 'Insanely risky.'

'It's all we have because of the time constraints,' Bodie said. 'We're up against it here. If you could meet the gang tomorrow, we could have Garpo by the evening.'

Heidi shook her head. 'That's the best-case scenario,' she said. 'Things don't go that smoothly in real life.'

Bodie shrugged. 'We make the best of it. This team *is* the best. I know you two can do it.'

Heidi looked at Yasmine. 'I guess we both have the experience of undercover work. That part won't be hard.'

'Lots of things could go wrong,' Lucie said. 'There's an infinite number of variables at play.'

Bodie nodded. He looked at Heidi and Yasmine. They both looked positive. 'We can deal with anything,' Heidi said. 'Once we're inside, we can say Garpo's an old contact or something. Try to get close.'

'Find out where he works and what he does,' Reilly said.

Heidi nodded, her eyes thoughtful. 'The more I think about it, the more I think we can do it,' she said and turned to Bodie. 'Make the call to Pantera.'

Bodie smiled and laid his hand on hers. 'I'll do it now.'

He made the call. Pantera answered quickly and listened hard. Soon, Bodie had hung up the phone, and they were all staring at each other.

'The die is cast,' Bodie said. 'Now we wait.'

CHAPTER FIFTEEN

The next morning, Heidi got a call on her phone. The number was unknown. She sat up in bed, nudged Bodie, and answered.

'Hello?'

'Is that Heidi?' a breathy voice asked.

'Yes, that's me.'

'My name is Frank. I work for the Skaya. We're told you want to do some work for us.'

Heidi cleared her throat. 'We do. I didn't expect you to make contact so quickly.'

'I'm told you have a partner?'

'Yes, it's me and Yasmine.'

'Time is of the essence. Can you come to a meeting?'

Heidi swung her legs out of bed. 'Of course we can. When did you have in mind?'

'Noon.' He reeled off an address. 'Just you two. Nobody else. We will see if we like you.'

The line went dead. Heidi repeated the conversation for Bodie. 'I don't like it,' she said. 'The guy almost sounded desperate.'

Bodie nodded, getting dressed. 'It's all a bit sudden,' he said. 'But it's just what we wanted. It's the introduction.'

They arranged to meet the others downstairs. Soon they were eating breakfast and engaged in conversation. It was nine thirty. Two and a half hours before the meet was scheduled. It had all come around very quickly.

'Pantera has presented you two as world-class thieves,' Bodie told everyone. 'He told the Skaya you're lucky to be on the market, so to speak. I think that's why they've jumped for you.'

Heidi took a deep breath. 'It is what it is,' she said. 'We're ready.'

The time passed quickly. Thirty minutes before noon, Heidi and Cassidy climbed into a taxi and left the others behind. They were on their way to the meeting with the notorious Skaya gang. Heidi stared out the window, taking none of it in.

'You good with this?' Yasmine asked her.

'It's been a while,' Heidi admitted. 'I'm a little nervous.'

'I'll take the lead. It's second nature to me.'

Heidi nodded. The taxi took them through a maze of back streets where dogs roamed and children played and groups of people stood on street corners. It seemed greyer down here, as if the sun feared the place. Heidi swallowed as the taxi came to a halt.

The driver pointed across the street. 'Number thirteen,' he said with an accent. Heidi paid him and then they got out into a warm day, the breeze barely there. They stood for a moment on the kerb, looking both ways, and then crossed. They walked up to a grim concrete building with a harsh façade, rusted bars across its windows, and a heavy steel front door. The rest of the block looked similar, all bland, ugly-looking buildings with no joy.

Yasmine took the lead and knocked. The door was immediately opened by a hatchet faced man with a bald pate and squinty eyes. He stared at them.

'Yasmine and Heidi,' Yasmine said. 'Here for the meeting.'

The man nodded. He stepped past them, looked up and down the street. He looked for a while before grunting and then stepping back inside the building.

'Follow me.'

Heidi realised the front door led onto a row of offices that opened along a wide corridor, windows to both sides. They traversed the corridor quickly, ending up at a wooden door at the very end. The hatchet faced guy knocked on the door.

'They're here, boss,' he said.

There was a yell of affirmation. Their guide opened the door and waved them in. Heidi followed Yasmine into a large, wide office. It was furnished with paintings of animals on the wall and a plush grey carpet. There was an extensive oak desk, a drinks cabinet and another desk with a computer monitor to the right, a row of filing cabinets to the left. There were a couple of bronze statues in the corners.

Three men were in the room. One sat behind the desk and the other two stood on either side of him. All men wore glasses and suits and looked like business executives. The one seated behind the desk waved the two women inside.

'Please, take a seat. I am Petrov, the man who called you. You two come with a very big reputation.'

Heidi settled into the soft leather chair. She let Yasmine take the lead, appearing nonchalant.

'That's good to hear,' Yasmine said. 'We do our best.'

'What can you do?'

'Yeah, do you give any extras?' The man on the left said in a sleazy voice.

Yasmine looked at him coldly. 'We provide our skills as a service,' she said. 'Nothing else. You provide a job, we carry it out, we get paid. We're not part of your gang. But you will be glad you have us.'

'I'd like to have you,' the man on the left went on. 'All night.'

Petrov raised an impatient hand. 'Stop it, Alex. We're here for business. Important business,' he stared at them. 'You know you're going to have to prove yourselves to us.'

'That shouldn't be a problem,' Yasmine said.

'And fit in with the team,' Alex said.

Yasmine gave them a concerned look. 'We normally work alone. Just the two of us.'

'That's possible,' Petrov said. 'But, occasionally, it will be a team.'

Yasmine looked like she was considering it. 'Well, it could work,' she said. 'We know some of your people.'

Pantera had given them some names.

'You do?' Petrov asked. 'Who do you know?'

'Garpo mostly,' Yasmine said. 'But Taran and Yusupov too. And Umarov. Not very well, I might add.'

Petrov nodded. 'You know Garpo? How do you know him?'

'How *well* do you know him?' Alex smirked. 'Garpo has a reputation.'

'Not that well,' Yasmine admitted. 'We did a job once, that's all.'

Petrov nodded and turned his attention to Heidi. 'And you? Do you talk?'

'As little as possible,' Heidi gave him a smile and leaned forward. 'I'm the quiet one.'

'I'd find a way to make you-' Alex began, but Petrov raised another impatient hand.

'Stop it,' he barked. 'We need them for the job. Stop acting the fool.'

Alex clammed up. Heidi wanted to jump over the desk and introduce him to her knuckles. Instead, she smiled and kept her mouth shut.

'Job?' Yasmine said enquiringly. 'You have one already?' Heidi felt her mouth go dry.

'Immediate start,' Petrov said with a smile. 'And test. What do you say? Are you ready to start working for the Skaya straight away?'

Yasmine cleared her throat to hide any discomfort. 'I guess so.'

'You sound surprised?'

'I'm surprised you would trust us so quickly.'

'It's not you. It's the person who recommended you. And this, as I said, will be a test. We'll see how good you are tonight.'

Heidi could tell Alex wanted to add something salacious, but forced it down. Yasmine crossed her legs and leaned back.

'So let's hear more,' she said. 'What job do you want us to do?'

'Two high end cars,' Petrov said. 'They're being stored in a warehouse and belong to a rival of ours. We want to steal the cars to send a message. All we want is for you to steal them. We'll torch them later and leave them somewhere poignant,' he laughed. 'The warehouse will be well guarded. Do you think you can get in, get the cars, and get out?'

'It will take a few weeks of planning,' Heidi said.

'We want you to do it tonight.'

Yasmine didn't have to look shocked. 'Tonight? Are you kidding?'

Petrov spread his hands. 'I thought you were the best.'

There were several moments of cold tension. Heidi let Yasmine handle it. She knew the stakes.

'A job like this would normally take lots of planning,' Yasmine reiterated. 'We stake the place out. We get inside if we can. You locate the alarm systems and the CCTV if there are any. You figure out the guards' rotas. There's a dry run, surveillance, planning. You cover every aspect. And you want us to go in *tonight?*'

Petrov spread his hands. 'That's how you get in bed with the big boys.'

Alex smirked. Yasmine looked briefly at Heidi, her eyes wide. 'Well,' she said. 'If that's what we have to do.'

She turned back to Petrov. 'Let's have the details.'

CHAPTER SIXTEEN

Heidi crouched low, deep in shadow, behind a row of bushes. Yasmine was at her side. The two women were comfortably ensconced across the street from the warehouse that housed the high end cars. The warehouse was a squat, brick building with wide roller shutter doors out front and two normal side doors to the right. Its roof was sharply angled. It was a two-storey affair and had a row of windows across the top level. Shadows passed the windows every so often, and men came out of the side doors to smoke. Heidi and Yasmine had determined there were at least four guards inside, maybe more. The men were armed and tough looking.

Heidi checked the time. 'Almost midnight. We'll give them a little longer to get sleepier.'

Ten minutes later, there was movement across the way. One guard left the warehouse, got into a parked car, and left.

'Maybe he's going for takeout,' Yasmine said.

'Or his shift's finished,' Heidi said. 'It's not time yet, anyway.'

The guard didn't return. Half past midnight became 1 a.m. and still they waited. The night grew chilly around them.

When Heidi's watch read a quarter past two, she shifted. 'You ready?'

'As I'll ever be.'

They started moving. They wore dark clothing, hats to help cover their faces, and thin gloves for the fingerprints. There were no more words. Instinctively, they both knew what to do. It was a shame that the best and most experienced thieves in their group, Bodie, Cassidy and Jemma, weren't the ones doing this.

Heidi reached the far door, the one they hadn't seen used all night, and pressed her back against the wall beside it. Yasmine joined her. Heidi reached for the handle, twisted it, found it locked. That was actually a good thing. It meant nobody used it. She took out a set of lock picks and went to work.

'It's been a while,' she said.

'They teach you that stuff in the CIA?'

'First day.'

It took a few minutes, and then the lock gave. Heidi eased open the door and peered inside. It was a small service room, full of boxes and domestic appliances. Heidi and Yasmine went in, closing the door behind them. They paused for a while, listening.

They heard a brief murmur of conversation echoing around a large space. They heard footsteps pass by. Nothing else. Heidi went to the far door.

Carefully, she opened it. The warehouse proper now stood in front of her, a wide space with offices around the edges, occupied by piles of boxes and car parts, excess pizza boxes and tables around which the men could sit and eat and drink. One man had his feet up on a chair as they watched, guzzling on something from a dark bottle. Heidi also saw another man patrolling the space, looking bored out of his skull.

And now she saw the two high-end vehicles they had come to steal. 'Nice,' Heidi said.

One was an older model Ferrari 308GTB in red. The other was a deep blue Ferrari Purosangue that looked brand new.

Still the women didn't speak. They knew what needed doing.

Finally, Heidi said, 'You sort it upstairs. I'll sort it down here.'

'You got two to deal with,' Yasmine said.

Heidi nodded. Yasmine slipped into the warehouse and stayed low, padding for a set of stairs on the far right. She took her time as Heidi watched. The guards were complacent and never noticed the movement. Soon, Yasmine was out of sight.

It was Heidi's turn.

The guards on the ground floor weren't close together, and they weren't facing each other. She chose the one sitting down first and stalked out of the service room, stealing across the floor, making a beeline for him. She stayed behind piles of boxes as she got closer, keeping her eye on the other patrolling guard.

She was three feet away from her target. The man tipped his bottle back and drank deeply. He sighed, bored. Heidi stepped out of concealment and ran lightly over to him, slipped an arm around his throat and choked him out.

He struggled. His feet kicked at the floor. He leaned back into her. Heidi held on tight and squeezed with just the right amount of strength. She held him as quietly as she could. He fought back, but finally slumped.

His last act was to kick the table.

The noise echoed around the warehouse. Heidi froze. The other guard was busy flicking through his phone and didn't look over.

She grabbed the guard's gun and pointed it at the other guard. 'Hands up,' she said.

The man turned and didn't bat an eyelid. He still looked bored. 'What the hell do you want?' he asked.

Heidi didn't speak. She stalked over to him. 'Lay the gun on the floor.'

He did so, taking it slow. He held his hands in the air without being asked. The man actually seemed pleased to be relieving the boredom. Heidi scooped up his gun and stuffed it into her waistband.

'Don't move.'

She waited. Three minutes later, Yasmine returned, walking down the stairs alone. She gave Heidi a thumbs up. 'One upstairs,' she said. 'Taken care of. Even managed to tie him up.'

She produced a set of zip ties and threw them to Heidi.

'Where the hell did you find those?'

'The guy was carrying them,' Yasmine shrugged. 'It always pays to search them.'

Heidi zip tied her guard and pointed her gun at his head. 'The keys to the cars,' she said. 'Where are they?'

He shook his head, and now there was fear in his eyes. 'I can't tell you.'

Heidi aimed the gun at his thigh. 'I'll start by

shooting you in the legs, then the arms, and then we'll get on to deadlier places.'

The guard licked his lips. 'Please.'

'What the hell are you all guarding, anyway?' Yasmine asked. 'Three armed guards for two cars seems over the top to me.'

The guard swallowed. 'I can't tell you that either.'

Heidi waved the gun. 'Keys?'

The guard glanced quickly at one of the offices, then looked away. Heidi saw which one, gave the gun to Yasmine, and said, 'Cover him for me.'

She ran over to the office and looked inside. Right there, on the wall, were two rows of hooks. Car keys hung from two. Heidi plucked them free and ran back into the warehouse.

'Got 'em.'

Yasmine looked at the guard. 'What are we gonna do with him?'

Heidi didn't hesitate. 'We can't just leave him like this. Choke him out.'

Yasmine coughed. 'I've got the gun.'

Heidi pocketed the keys and walked up to the guard, who looked suddenly scared. 'You don't have to do that,' he said. 'I'll be quiet. I won't try to stop you.'

'We know,' Heidi said.

She stepped around him, grabbed him, and started to choke. The guy struggled hard, not wanting the indignity. Heidi held him tight and didn't let up. It didn't take long. Soon, the guy was slumping at her feet.

She looked around at the cars. 'Shall we?'

Yasmine nodded. 'Well, that all went rather-'

'Hold it,' a voice said, splitting through the warehouse's stillness. 'Put your guns down. What are you doing here?'

Heidi cursed and turned to the side door. A man stood there. The same man who'd departed earlier. He held a large box in one hand and a gun in the other. He looked startled.

Both Heidi and Yasmine walked towards him. They got within eight feet before he realised what they were doing and started waving the gun. 'Stop that. Stay there. Don't move.'

Heidi stopped. She still held the gun, low down her thigh, pointed at the ground. She saw the new guard's gun hand shaking. These weren't seasoned veterans of the gang, by any means.

'Are you guarding the cars too?' Yasmine asked, just to keep the guy off balance.

His mouth opened, but nothing came out.

'I'd put that box down if I were you,' Heidi said. 'It'll affect your aim.'

Trying to sow doubts in his mind.

The man's eyes flickered to the box. It looked heavy. His left bicep was shaking with the strain.

He stepped back, started to bend from the waist. As he did so, his gaze left them and went to the box. Heidi acted instantly. She brought her gun up and leapt in, smashing him across the face. He yelled and brought his own gun up. The weapon discharged over her right shoulder.

Yasmine ran in from the left. She smashed her gun across the man's head, staggering him. Heidi already had hold of his gun arm and was keeping it straight, the weapon harmless.

'Drop it,' Yasmine yelled, threatening him with the gun again.

He didn't, just continued to struggle. Yasmine didn't give him an inch. She smashed him across the face. Blood flew from his torn cheek. The guy's eyes were wide, his mouth making a series of groans. His teeth were bloody.

Heidi dropped her own gun, then brought her fingers to bear on the guy's wrist. She broke it. The gun fell to the floor. The guy's breath whistled between his teeth. Heidi elbowed him in the throat.

Now the man crumpled. Yasmine stepped around him and choked him out, too. Now they had four downed guards. Heidi looked around at their handiwork and then glanced at the two cars.

'I can't use stick,' she said. 'That old Ferrari's all stick. Can you drive it?'

Yasmine nodded. 'I can.'

'Then I'll take the blue one. It's a new model, so should be an auto.'

They dashed for the cars, but checked on the guards first. All were alive and sprawled out, breathing softly, tied in place. Heidi hated to think what would happen to them when their bosses found out what had happened, but she couldn't worry about that. They'd got the cars and would now have to deliver them to Petrov.

They climbed into the vehicles, started them, and then raised the roller shutter door. They drove out into the night.

It was a job well done, a job well deserved. Heidi's car purred beneath her as if it welcomed her presence. She handled it well and kept below the speed limit all the way to the predetermined meeting point.

When they arrived, there were people waiting for her. One of them was Petrov.

He was grinning. 'Fantastic job,' he said.

CHAPTER SEVENTEEN

Petrov loved them. He congratulated them at the meet point and then insisted that they come back to the office. Once there, he sat them down and poured drinks. It was just Petrov and Alex, no guards. Petrov toasted to a great night.

'To the future,' Petrov said.

'My only concern is for those beautiful cars,' Heidi said. 'Especially the 308.'

'You know your cars?' Petrov asked.

'Even sexier,' Alex said.

Heidi nodded. 'I do.'

'The guys will love you,' Petrov said. 'Good at your job. Sexy. And you can talk about cars. You should go to the clubs.'

Heidi leaned forward. 'Which clubs?'

Petrov took a big gulp of his drink. 'There are a few we Skaya frequent. Rosario's, not too far from here. And Tremolow's. A few miles to the east.'

'Do all the Skaya go there?' Heidi asked, finishing her drink.

Petrov refilled it. 'All those who want to, or are within distance. There are other HQs around the city that have their own clubs.'

'But we can go to those two?' Yasmine asked.

'Of course. The guys would love it. You're in now. Not in the mafia, of course,' he laughed. 'But in the organisation we operate.'

'I'd love to go to a club,' Yasmine said. 'We had to choke four guards out tonight. I'm wired.'

Everyone laughed, even Alex, who had been looking a little subdued. 'I could take you,' he said hopefully. 'Get you through the doors.'

'Oh, yeah, because I just love your sex talk,' Yasmine laughed.

They all laughed. The women were talking themselves deeper into the men's trust. If they were willing to go to the clubs, they might become bigger players in the organisation. They would fit in better.

'How about right now?' Petrov said. 'How about we all go? It will be fun.'

Heidi checked her watch. 'Is it twenty-four hours?'

Petrov nodded. 'We go all day and all night. Just like the men.'

Yasmine finished her drink and then rose to her feet. 'Take me,' she said playfully. 'I'm yours.'

Soon, they were in the back of Petrov's big Mercedes, winging their way to the nearest club, which was Romero's. The black car pulled up outside, the door opened, and the interior was suddenly flooded with noise. The pavements were filled with partygoers even at this time of night. A line stretched from the front doors of Romero's, men and women dressed in all manner of ways. Heidi saw them smoking, drinking from hip flasks, surreptitiously snorting from the backs of their hands. She saw bare legs and arms and chests. Music spilled from the club onto the pavement, making some people dance in line. It was a lively party atmosphere, and there was no sign of it winding down.

Heidi and Yasmine climbed out of the back of the car. They waited for Petrov and Alex. Soon the men were there and leading them towards the front doors of the club. Petrov went straight up to the doorman.

He didn't speak. The doorman saw him, nodded and stepped aside. Heidi was conscious of a dozen jealous glances.

Inside, the club was bouncing. It was one huge room, filled with noise. Flashing lights roamed over everyone who was standing and gyrating inside, briefly illuminating them before passing on. Heidi saw two bars and numerous stages and several dancing poles. She saw hundreds of people with drinks in their hands, two ten-person-deep bars, and several curtained off areas.

Petrov yelled above the noise. 'Follow me.'

They made their way through the tumult. It wasn't easy and twice they almost lost Petrov. Alex stayed close, always watching. They arrived at the far side of the nightclub where the curtains were. Petrov glanced behind one, shut it, and then went to a second. He must have liked what he saw because his arms went wide and he enfolded someone in a hug. He pulled Heidi and Yasmine through and then told Alex to get them an enormous bottle of champagne.

'Tonight,' he said. 'We celebrate.'

Heidi found herself in a wide semi-circular room, facing a wide semi-circular couch. Men and women were sprawled across it. She counted twelve. Petrov stood before them, beaming.

'Here are our friends,' he said, meaning the Skaya.

'Friends, this is Heidi and Yasmine. Tonight, they have proven themselves worthy.'

The men unfolded themselves and came over, shaking hands. The women stayed put and nodded and smiled. Heidi noticed several of the men glancing appreciatively at her and Yasmine and knew they stood a chance at a more detailed conversation. These were men they could easily interrogate, and this was the place and time to do it.

She played her part, leaning into them when they talked, putting a hand on their arms. Heidi sipped her champagne, sat near Petrov, and joined in all their conversations. She spoke to a guy named Olly, and another named Jacques. A woman named Eliina joined in and then a man named Anatoly. It was a varied light conversation about anything that came to mind and it was fuelled by vodka and a little white powder. Heidi and Yasmine stayed well away from the substance, but they accepted the drinks that Petrov's people continued to ply them with.

It was very late when Petrov grabbed Heidi's attention and she managed to pull away from the inebriated, bearded man who had just bought her a drink.

'I may have another job for you,' Petrov said, mostly drunk. 'Give me a contact number.'

Heidi and Yasmine had both thought of that possibility before the night began, and Heidi fished her phone out of her pants. She exchanged numbers with Petrov. Now, they were all the way in.

She let the night unfold until, outside, there would be a hint of dawn on the horizon. It was only then, when everyone around her was three sheets to the wind, that she brought up Garpo again.

She couldn't remember the name of her latest suitor, but she leaned in with him. 'I worked with Garpo before,' she said. 'Do you know him?'

The man shook his head. Heidi moved past him, moved on to the next. All the men were willing to engage with her, even those with women on their arms.

'Garpo,' she said again. 'I worked with him once. Do you know him?'

Every time she said it, she made sure she was out of earshot of Petrov and Alex. She worked her way down the line of men.

At the fifth attempt, a look of recognition came into the man's eyes. This was an older man, swarthy, with salt and pepper hair and thick neck muscles. He nodded when Heidi mentioned the name Garpo.

'Ah, yes, I know him. He still works for us.'

'He does?' Heidi looked surprised and looked expectant.

'Yes, he deals with the...' the man clammed up and waved a little packet of white powder at her. 'Up on the east side. He wouldn't come here. Too far. He would go to Leonardo's over there.'

'I see. Well, maybe I'll go see him sometime.'

'He's a lucky man.' The guy, the fourth that night, put a meaty hand on her thigh.

Heidi laughed and got to her feet. She didn't fend the hand away, but her movement did the job. She made her way back to Yasmine. It took her a few moments to find the right time to lean over and whisper in her ear.

'Got it.'

Yasmine looked at her. 'Here?'

'No. A club on the east side. We'll have to go tomorrow now.'

'Then we go tomorrow and ask around. Someone will know Garpo.'

Heidi nodded. Their job here was done. She looked over at Petrov. The guy was looking decidedly the worse for wear.

Heidi leaned in to him, putting her own hand on his knee. 'Hey,' she said. 'We're gonna get out of here. It's late. Thanks for the evening.'

'Thanks for the cars,' Petrov said. 'I'll be in touch.'

Heidi nodded. Out of the corner of her eye she could see Alex looking jealous. She pulled away from Petrov.

'We'll be waiting for your call.'

Heidi and Yasmine rose to their feet, turned away from the table and made their way through the club. Heidi looked at Yasmine. They were both a bit drunk. They leaned on each other and soon found themselves outside at the side of the road.

A line of taxis was waiting.

Heidi and Yasmine jumped into the nearest and gave the driver the name of their hotel. Soon, they were driving through the city and towards relative safety. The pressure and the tension of the last few hours could dissolve.

Heidi settled back in the car seat, thinking about Garpo.

Tomorrow, they would go for him.

CHAPTER EIGHTEEN

Heidi thought the hour was ridiculously early the next morning when her phone beeped. It was actually ten thirty a.m., but it felt like three in the morning. Of course, she'd only been asleep for a couple of hours.

She raised her foggy head from the pillow and looked over at the nightstand. The screen on her phone was lit. She'd received a text message. Heidi licked her lips. Her mouth was dry, her throat parched. She had a headache. Too much alcohol. But it was also too early to function.

But the message could be important. She forced herself to raise her head, reach out for the phone, and bring it close to her face. At first, she couldn't focus, but slowly the letters arranged themselves.

Job available. Meet two p.m. for details. Petrov.

Heidi almost shook her head, but decided that would be a mistake. She had hoped for a day or twos grace, enough time to get to Garpo and then get the hell out of there. But it seemed they had made too good of an impression.

Damn.

She sat up in bed and rubbed her tired eyes. She needed water. Bodie wasn't there. He was probably downstairs, eating breakfast or chatting. He knew what time she'd rolled in and had left her to sleep. She threw her legs out of bed and grabbed some bottled water that was on the table by the window, chugged it down.

Heidi spent the rest of the morning catching the rest of the team up on developments. She ate breakfast, drank four coffees, and started to feel a little better. She drank copious amounts of water. Some time before twelve, Yasmine joined them. She looked even worse than Heidi.

'This afternoon?' She groaned when she found out. 'Oh, no. I need to go back to bed.'

The two women rallied, finding their energy. By one, they were ready to head out. Heidi ordered a taxi to take them to an address Petrov texted them and soon they were on their way, seeing more of the city. It was a drab, overcast day that promised nothing but cold showers. People wandered along the street in coats and hats and carried umbrellas. The elements matched Heidi's mood.

Petrov was waiting for them in a large office inside another office block. Alex was at his side. Both men looked fresh and ready to go. They were probably used to the late nights drinking and taking drugs. Or, Heidi thought, maybe they'd partaken of more drugs to bring them around faster that morning.

'Did you enjoy our partying last night?' Petrov asked first.

'I may have got a little drunk,' Yasmine said with a smile, again taking the lead. 'I can't remember a good chunk of it.'

'It is the same every night,' Alex said. 'We like to party hard.'

'Well, tonight, we're out,' Yasmine said. 'I need my beauty sleep at least every other night.'

Alex looked sad. 'That is disappointing. We like fresh blood.'

Petrov looked impatient. 'Well, let's get to the business,' he said. 'As I said, we have a job. It's tricky, and you two came to mind immediately.' He went on to describe the job in depth, which included breaking into a military warehouse and stealing a particular cache of advanced weapons. The job would be worth millions to the mafia.

'I can cut you in on a little of that,' he said.

Yasmine spoke up. 'Do we have time to plan this one?'

Petrov laughed. 'Of course, we don't expect it to happen immediately. You need to go away and plan. You need the details. The layout, the information. I understand. I can give you all that, and then you go plan. Yes?'

Yasmine nodded. 'We can handle that.'

Petrov proceeded to give them an A4 folder with lots of pages inside. He tapped it on the table. 'I am trusting you now,' he said. 'This is all the information we have. It's not the only copy, but look after it. I'd like your initial thoughts in a day or two.'

Heidi took the folder. Yasmine said, 'That's fair.'

They rose to their feet and left Petrov's office. Alex tried to get them to attend the club that night again, but there was no chance of that. They had other plans and politely turned Alex down. Then they were in the taxi headed back for the hotel, folder in hand.

'We got deep fast,' Heidi said. 'Deep in their organisation, I mean.'

'Too deep, too fast,' Yasmine sighed. 'But tonight is important.'

'Yeah, let's concentrate on that.'

They spent the rest of the day talking to the team and perusing Petrov's files so, later, they could inform the authorities of the potential threat, and then got ready to go out. Heidi pulled on the same dress as the night before and sat in front of the mirror, doing her makeup. She made sure Bodie had her temporary phone number and then hugged him in the middle of the room.

'Wish me luck.'

He did, and he hugged her, and then she was on her way. She met Yasmine in the lobby. The two women were all dressed up and ready for a night on the town. Only, they weren't going into town.

Heidi grabbed a taxi and gave him the name of the nightclub they were headed for. 'Leonardo's' she said.

The guy nodded and set off. Half an hour later, he pulled up at the kerb and let them out. There was no missing Leonardo's.

There was a big flashing sign above the door outside, and a comparatively short queue to get in. It was relatively early, the full evening crowd not kicking in yet. Heidi and Yasmine joined it and waited their turn. It was noisy; the air filled with conversation. Heidi and Yasmine did their best not to get drawn into any of it.

Twenty minutes later, they were inside the club. Heidi decided they needed to get their bearings, so they went over to the bar, ordered a drink, and stood there for a while, taking in everything around them. The dance floor was enormous. Cages hung far to the left, where select people were allowed to sway. The bar occupied the entire right side of the club and was also extensive. At the far side, Heidi could see a row of booths, two with curtains across and five without. Men and women sat chatting and drinking in all of them. Heidi saw security to left and right and several servers cutting through the crowds carrying trays of drinks. They were experts at avoiding collision.

'You think he'll be here yet?' Yasmine asked, raising her voice above the music.

'Can't say. But we'll only have one shot at asking for him. Let's wait a while.'

They idled the time away, not drinking heavily, just sipping. They kept their eyes on the booths and saw more men and women arrive. Nobody left. The area was filling up. Heidi waited until midnight and then decided it was time to move.

'Let's do it,' she said.

They deposited their empty glasses on the bar and made their way through the crowds towards the booths. It was hard going. Eventually, they twisted their way around the last gaggle of people and faced the booths. The people inside looked highly inebriated.

Heidi singled out a man sitting mostly on his own and approached him. 'Do you know Garpo?' she asked.

She sat down next to him invitingly. He stared at her. She was aware of Yasmine approaching someone else. They needed to be careful with this.

'Garpo,' she said. 'I was told to find Garpo by Petrov.'

Recognition flashed in the man's eyes, but then he shook his head. 'I don't know any Garpo,' he said.

Heidi nodded and moved on to the next target. She was surprised the man didn't know. This was Garpo's hangout, and the man had clearly recognised Petrov's name. Maybe he hadn't wanted to get involved.

She approached a young woman, asked the same question of her and the man seated beside her. They both nodded.

'Garpo is there,' the man said. 'With all the chains.'

He pointed. Heidi followed his finger to see a man wearing an open shirt and dress trousers. His shoes were shiny. Around his neck were draped half a dozen golden chains that swayed whenever he moved. His black hair was slicked back.

Heidi sighed inwardly. They had come a long way to find this man, gone through a lot. And here he was. Inside a nightclub, partying, larger than life. It was a relief to see him.

Heidi thanked the couple and caught Yasmine's eye. She nodded at Garpo. The two women rose and approached him.

He was drinking when they got to him, tipping a tumbler back and emptying the contents. When he saw them, his eyes widened.

'Are you Garpo?' Heidi wasted no time.

'Yes, that is me,' his accent was heavy and hesitant. 'Do you want to sleep with me?'

'Not tonight,' Yasmine said. 'We have a few questions for you.'

And right then, she knew she'd made a mistake.

CHAPTER NINETEEN

Garpo's eyes narrowed, and a look of mistrust crossed his face. 'You want to question me? Are you the cops?'

Yasmine laughed, trying to cover her mistake. 'No, no, nothing like that. We work for Petrov.'

'Really? And what does Petrov have two beautiful creatures as yourself doing?'

'We can't say exactly,' Heidi said with a small smile. 'But he's enjoying it. He gave us a big job this afternoon.'

Garpo's eyes narrowed. He looked past the two women as if seeking assistance. For now, though, he didn't move.

'Did Petrov send you to ask me questions?' he asked suspiciously.

'No, nothing like that. It's something else we heard from a contact,' Heidi forged ahead, thinking there was no time like the present. 'What do you know about the funerary mask of Tutankhamun being stolen?'

Garpo blinked. His mouth clammed up, and he stared at them. It appeared that he didn't know what to say. Again, he looked beyond them.

Finally, words came. 'Are you joking? Is this a

joke?' He looked around, as if expecting a friend to jump out and confess.

'No joke,' Heidi said with lightness in her voice. 'You see, we've heard the same. And we're thieves, so we're interested. We just need to find out who's behind it so we can make contact.'

'Tutankhamun's mask?'

'Yeah, you told someone it was going to be stolen.'

Now Garpo's eyes really narrowed, and he made a decision. He shouted past Heidi's shoulder, shouted for help.

'We have rats,' he cried. 'Help me.'

And, with no more ado and with total surprise, he waded in.

Heidi was shocked as Garpo stepped in and swung at her. He aimed for her head. She ducked at the last moment, but the blow still glanced off her skull. It stung. She tried to rescue the situation, holding her hands up.

'Wait, wait, this isn't what we-'

Garpo was having none of it. He swung again, aiming for her midriff. Heidi had nowhere to go. She blocked the punch, still reluctant to fight back. At her side, Yasmine was checking to see who was coming to Garpo's aid.

So far, all the men were still seated and staring at Garpo as if he might be joking, or mad. When he started swinging, one of them rose to his feet. Yasmine went over to him, smiling, and told him it was a bit of fun. Nothing serious. But the man's eyes told her he wasn't accepting it. The only reason he was still half-seated was because he was half drunk.

Heidi blocked another punch and then caught

Garpo's wrist. 'All right, all right,' she said. 'Back off. We were just looking for business.'

But Garpo wasn't having it. He wrenched his arm back and then waded in again, and now he was shouting for help.

'Come on, you guys,' he cried. 'Help me with these two. They're either cops or rats.'

The mention of the word 'cops' galvanised everyone. Men surged to their feet and started towards the skirmish.

Yasmine stood in the way of four men. Now, the gloves were well and truly off. They were in trouble. She took advantage of their drunken state, letting them get close and then smashing the first in the throat. She punched the next one in the nose, but the third was ready for her. Two men were already on their knees to her left and right. The third caught her kick and deflected it. The fourth came around him.

Garpo attacked Heidi with everything he had. It wasn't enough. Heidi fended him off with ease and, seeing Yasmine's predicament, started to hit back properly. Garpo went to his knees, and Heidi saw an opportunity.

She bent over and clutched his throat. 'Tell me who told you about the mask,' she whispered vehemently.

Garpo gasped. Heidi punched him in the cheek. She gripped his throat. 'Tell me now.'

Garpo struggled. |Heidi glanced over to Yasmine. She'd floored two men but was now fighting two more. Others were coming from another booth. They were vastly outnumbered, and had to get the hell away from here.

'Yas,' she yelled. 'Run.'

Yasmine turned, and then a man flung himself at her. She stumbled and fell to her knees before him. He tried to swipe at her, but missed. She was now at a disadvantage as three more men appeared.

Heidi knew she had to help. She'd incapacitate Garpo and rush to Yasmine's aid. She turned to do just that and Garpo chose that moment to surge up. By luck, the top of his head connected with the bottom of her chin. Suddenly, she saw black spots. Her body went weak. She fell backwards, across the nearest table.

She was still alert, but befuddled. Her arms wouldn't work, her legs lay uselessly. Garpo threw himself on her and started punching. Heidi felt the blows, struggled.

The pain was actually helping her come around. Her head cleared. Garpo was punching her stomach, her ribs. She could see Yasmine struggling past the next table. She had to negate Garpo and go help her friend.

Heidi gripped Garpo's exposed throat in two hands and squeezed. Immediately, he stopped punching her and tried to break her grip. She didn't let up. Garpo's eyes bulged. He went red, and then purple. This was no choke hold. She didn't want to choke him out.

This was real.

Garpo batted at her ineffectually. He was growing weaker by the second. He beat his hands at her inadequately. Heidi maintained her grip until the last possible second.

And then she let go. Garpo collapsed at her side,

slumped and barely breathing, as Heidi struggled to her feet. She hung her head, raised it, and took in her surroundings.

Yasmine fought two men. Two others were climbing to their feet. Four more were headed for the fight. They had to cut loose and run. She rushed over to Yasmine's side. A man lunged. Heidi blocked his attack and kicked out, sending him sprawling across the couch. A woman, looking unhappy, then flung herself at Heidi. She came in low and fast. Heidi kneed her in the face and grabbed Yasmine's arm.

'Let's go.'

They disengaged from the fight, but they didn't have the time to escape. Already, the other four men were upon them. The nightclub was still bouncing, but a gap had cleared around them. There was no panic.

The four men surrounded Heidi and Yasmine, and now the first four had staggered upright. By now, Garpo was also on his feet, rubbing his throat.

'Who are you?' He gasped, coming towards them. *'Who are you?'*

Heidi stepped back, but there were two men behind her who pushed her back. 'I told you. We're looking for work.'

'Why do you want to know about the mask?'

'Seems like our kind of job. Look, there's no need for all this aggro.'

Faced with nine opponents, Heidi knew they had to talk their way out.

'You're gonna come with us,' Garpo said heatedly. 'We'll talk about what you really want.'

Heidi carefully thumbed the phone in her pocket,

pressed the speed dial for Bodie's number. After a few seconds, she said, 'We haven't done anything wrong.'

'You're coming with us.'

'Where are you taking us?'

'Somewhere a little quieter where we can have a little chat.'

'We could scream. Someone will call the police.'

Garpo laughed. 'This is our club. We make the rules.'

'The cops know better than to come here,' another man said with an evil little sneer.

Heidi looked at the men confronting her. Several of them were injured, holding themselves gingerly or standing in clear pain. They wouldn't last long if Heidi and Yasmine attacked hard. Garpo was a non-entity in a fight. Maybe...

Then the last sliver of hope died. Three more men appeared from a different couch, backing up the others. Heidi could see the odds were too much. She looked Garpo in the eye.

'We're telling you the truth,' she said. 'And we don't agree with you taking us from this place.'

Bodie would be hearing everything.

Garpo smirked. 'We'll see how your answers change under interrogation.'

Yasmine stiffened at Heidi's side. Maybe she was thinking about risking a fight anyway. It couldn't hurt to try. But it would hurt, Heidi thought. There were just too many enemies. She turned to Yasmine.

'Trust Bodie,' she whispered. 'He's aware.'

Yasmine nodded briefly.

Garpo gestured at Heidi and Yasmine. 'Take them.'

CHAPTER TWENTY

Outside the club, Bodie listened intently, knowing Heidi and Yasmine were in trouble. The entire team was listening, leaning forward. Bodie's phone was on speaker.

'Cover all the exit doors,' Bodie said quickly. 'Do it now.'

The team rushed out of the car. They'd already determined there were only two exits. The main front door, and one to the side. Cassidy and Reilly ran to that one, standing surreptitiously in the street. Bodie and the others stayed on the front.

They waited. There was no more chatter. Heidi and Yasmine were being forced to move against their will. Bodie had had high hopes for this operation. It had started so well with the car heist. But maybe they had overplayed their hand with Garpo. Maybe the guy was just plain suspicious. Or just plain dumb.

The chilly night air surrounded them. The loud voices of the slightly inebriated rose above everything else as the queue around the nightclub got bigger. Bodie and his team watched everything.

Minutes later, the side door burst open. Men rushed out. Bodie saw Heidi and Yasmine step out amid a gaggle of men and prepared himself. Just then, though, a car screeched up and stopped in the middle of the road. Heidi and Yasmine were bundled inside and then men squeezed alongside them. A second car pulled up behind. They were big, black vehicles with bright lights and gleaming chrome grills.

Garpo's men were quick. The entire operation took just seconds. The car's engines roared and soon they were moving, carrying Heidi and Yasmine to their fate. Bodie cursed and ran back to the car. Soon, Cassidy and Reilly had rejoined the team.

Bodie stayed behind the second car, letting it get ahead but not too far. He knew that this was desperate now. He couldn't lose the car. If he did, Heidi and Yasmine might die.

He breathed deeply, maintaining control. It wasn't easy. The others stayed silent, knowing what was at stake. They bypassed glittering restaurants and pubs and clubs outside which were massed crowds of people. They passed a busy transport hub, full of men and women hopping from place to place. The night lights were bright and the skies pitch black.

Bodie stayed on the vehicle's tail. The traffic went from sparse to thick as they traversed different streets and got stuck at lights. The car containing Heidi and Yasmine didn't seem in too much of a hurry, which was useful. It helped Bodie sustain his subterfuge.

They negotiated the streets, heading out of the city. Half an hour after they'd set off, they entered an industrial estate that was populated by dark office blocks and low warehouses. Here, there were no other cars, so Bodie backed off further and turned off his lights. He followed even more carefully now, giving the lead cars plenty of space.

Finally, they pulled up outside an office block. They parked at the side of the road. An exterior fence protected the office. Men climbed out of the two cars, and then they dragged Heidi and Yasmine out. Bodie had already come to a stop. The team observed. Heidi and Yasmine were pushed towards a gate in the fence and then prodded through. Bodie saw Heidi looking around. She wouldn't see him, and might think she and Yasmine were alone. He hoped not. Their situation looked hopeless.

Bodie counted nine men. One of them, probably Garpo, was gesticulating and issuing orders. The two women were led to the large front door. A man opened it, and then they were pushed through. Soon, all nine men and two women had disappeared inside, and the area was quiet again.

Bodie and the others slipped out of their car and went to investigate.

On closer inspection, the office block fronted what Bodie could only think of as a car jungle. It was a scrapyard, full of rows and heaps of rusting wrecks, piles upon piles. It looked unsafe even to the casual eye and was probably an eyesore to the neighbourhood. Bodie and the others crouched among some bushes across the road.

'We can't waste too much time,' Bodie whispered. 'We don't know what's happening inside.'

'It won't be anything good,' Cassidy said.

Bodie fretted at her words. He viewed the front door, then thought about the layout of the place.

There was a fence surrounding the entire lot, and it wasn't too clever at the back where the wrecks were kept. There was also a back door that looked old and weary. To be fair, he thought, there wasn't much choice. There were only two means of entry, since all the windows were barred.

'C'mon,' he said.

Carefully, the team made its way around the back, keeping to the shadows and bushes, the dark places. They blended in and took their time, allowing no misstep. They couldn't afford to make a mistake now.

Bodie found a large, decrepit area of fence that yielded easily to a few hard tugs. He peeled the chain-link back and crept inside. The others followed. Now they could easily hide among the wrecks as they made their way toward the back door.

Bodie crouched by a rusting hulk that formed the base of a rotting tower of four. He crept in the direction of the house. The only sounds were the distant humming of passing vehicles from a road miles away. Bodie's mouth was dry and when he swallowed his throat crackled. Gently, he laid a hand on the front end of one of the cars, balancing himself. The metal was cold and alien to the touch.

Finally, they reached the back door and crouched low, their backs to the wall. Bodie reached up and dealt with the lock. He turned to the others.

'Here we go.'

He rose, opened the door, and stepped inside, found himself in a small empty office. The team crept in. Bodie went to the door, listening. He could hear raised voices. His hand went to the door handle.

As it did, the handle turned. It all happened at

lightning speed. The door opened in and a man stepped through. He came face to face with Bodie and blinked, looking as shocked as Bodie was. There was a moment of inactivity.

Then, the man reached for the knife at his waist. His expression didn't change, but his eyes narrowed. He opened his mouth to let out a warning yell.

Bodie filled it with a fist. The man only grunted. One of his teeth broke. Bodie's knuckles bled. He caught the knife arm and broke it quickly, now cupping the guy's mouth so that he couldn't make a sound. Cassidy was on him too, bending the guy's other arm behind his back. Together, they subdued him quickly and dragged him into the empty room.

'What are we gonna do with him?' Lucie whispered.

Cassidy answered that question without words with a harsh punch to the temple. It only took one. The man's eyes closed and his head lolled. Cassidy dragged him into the corner.

'That leaves eight,' Bodie said.

He approached the door again, opened it. Outside, a narrow corridor led past several rooms. For now, it was empty.

He motioned for the others to stay where they were. It would be easier to seek Heidi and Yasmine out alone. Cassidy shook her head. 'Too dangerous to go alone,' she said. 'Like you said, there's still eight of them.'

Bodie acquiesced. She would accompany him. Together, they eased out into the corridor and stopped at the first room. Bodie peered through the window, saw an empty kitchen. The next window revealed a cluttered office, and so did the next. All were empty. Soon, they were at the end of the corridor, facing another door.

The angry voices were louder now.

Bodie looked down at the door handle, willing it to remain still. He didn't want a repeat of what had just happened. He reached out and twisted it, cracked the door open, and looked through the small gap.

Beyond, he saw a large office with a single desk and chair. It was huge. He also saw Yasmine and Heidi standing in the centre of the office in front of the desk. Their hands were tied behind their backs. They were facing the desk, behind which Garpo sat. He looked at ease now, lolling back and with his feet up on the desk. He was yelling at Heidi and Yasmine as his men stood to the sides. In his right hand he held a knife.

Bodie was relieved. Both women looked unharmed and stood easily. They hadn't been touched yet. Garpo looked like he was working his way up to it.

Right then, a man turned towards the door. Bodie eased it closed, gave Cassidy a quick sign. They crept back into one of the offices just in time. The door opened and a tall man with blonde hair stepped through. He headed straight for the kitchen.

Cassidy put a finger to her lips. Moving quickly and silently, she followed the man. She was a step behind him as he entered the kitchen. Once inside, she pounced. She drove a fist into his kidneys, displacing all his air, and then put him to the ground. He fell to his knees. Cassidy knocked him unconscious with two precise punches and then dragged him under the kitchen counter.

'Seven left,' she said when she returned to Bodie's side.

'All in that room,' he said. 'They're okay, but they won't be for long. Garpo's working himself up to something.'

'Then we attack,' Cassidy said. It was her 'go-to' mode.

This time Bodie was in agreement. 'Go get the others,' he said.

CHAPTER TWENTY ONE

It wasn't the best of plans, but there was no other way. They couldn't split up and go through the front door too, because there just wasn't time. Garpo looked like he really wanted to use that knife. Bodie couldn't risk it. Also, there was no other way into the big room apart from the two doors, one in front and one in back, and all the men were inside. They couldn't wait. They would have to attack in one shock and awe stream through a single door.

Bodie cracked the door again, just to double check he was right. Garpo was out of the chair now, brandishing the knife at Heidi. His face was set with a gleefully evil expression. Whatever he was going to do, he would enjoy.

'Are you ready?' Bodie heard him say.

He brought the knife up, and Heidi turned her head away. Yasmine snarled something. The men stood around came to attention, some of them watching intently, others almost turning their gazes away as if they didn't want to watch. Bodie raised a hand.

In the next second, he walked into the room as if he was the returning man. At first, nobody gave him a glance. Then Cassidy followed and then Reilly, and then the others, and Bodie rushed forward.

He threw himself at one man, head butting him in midair. The guy went down instantly, felled like a tree, covered in blood. Bodie didn't stop. His next opponent was Garpo himself, and this guy had a knife.

Flowing past him were Cassidy and Reilly, Jemma and Lucie, all joining the fight. They used the momentum of their surprise attack to gain a moment's advantage. They hit their enemies hard, knowing a quick knockout was imperative. Cassidy flew in with a right elbow to the face. Her opponent didn't even yell out; he collapsed to the floor in a groaning heap, his cheek shattered. The sound of breaking bone followed him down. Reilly didn't stand on ceremony. Running, he just launched a huge kick to his enemy's groin, folding him in half, and then landed on his head, leading with an elbow to send him in to oblivion. Lucie followed his lead, her kick striking dead centre, and then Jemma attacked with stiffened fingers to the throat, making her opponent clutch at himself with his hands and drop the knife he had been holding. He staggered back. Jemma grabbed hold of his head and smashed it into the wall, leaving a large dent in the plasterboard.

Bodie waited for Garpo's lunge. He watched the man closely. Garpo was clearly no knife fighter, he just felt confident with the weapon in hand. He flicked and swished it through the air, watching his men take a beating and looking intensely pissed.

'You work with these two?' He asked, slicing the knife left and right.

Bodie still didn't want to waste time. He had to deal with Garpo and then go help his team, maybe cut Heidi and Yasmine free. He needed to start the fight. Bodie feigned a lunge and then another. Garpo wasn't good enough to counter either. Bodie sighed inside. He was fighting a man so incompetent he wouldn't react properly. But Bodie couldn't get complacent. A knife was still a knife, a deadly weapon.

He stepped in, and Garpo finally attacked. The knife flashed. It sliced to Bodie's right, its owner overextended. Bodie capitalised on that mistake. He tried to break the arm, but couldn't get a proper grip. Garpo squirmed free.

'Who are you?' He said. 'What do you want?'

Again, Bodie didn't answer, anxious to get this over with. Garpo's men were fighting back. They had taken an initial beating, but most of them were tough and had not yielded. It was four versus five over there, and the bad guys knew they had the advantage. Cassidy and Reilly were still on top, but their opponents were taking up all their attention.

Bodie sidestepped a lunge that almost nicked Yasmine's ribcage. Now there was an opening. Bodie chopped hard at the wrist. The knife fell away and Garpo squealed. Bodie targeted his eyes and his nose, putting him on his knees. Then he scooped up the discarded knife.

In five seconds, he'd freed Heidi and Yasmine.

The women flexed their arms. Heidi walked up to Garpo and kicked him square in the chin. The man flew backwards, connecting roughly with the desk. He shook his head, looked up.

Heidi was standing before him. 'Bastard,' she said. 'You were going to cut us. You were looking forward to it. If we didn't need you, I'd kill you right now.'

Garpo looked afraid.

Heidi leaned down, now face to face. 'Tell me about the funerary mask,' she said.

Garpo swallowed heavily and opened his mouth, but at that moment his men rallied. One knocked Lucie off her feet, another forced Jemma back. The spare man attacked Reilly and sent him sprawling. Even Cassidy was beset, unable to make any headway.

The battle moved across the office, now close to the door through which Bodie had watched. The door opened. Yasmine ran to help. One of the bad guys slipped through the door into the hallway beyond. Cassidy followed. It was a free for all now.

Bodie left Heidi with Garpo and ran to help. The entire battle was leaving the room and filing into the hallway, where there was little space. It took the battle down to one on ones. Bodie was at the near end, looking for a man to fight but unable to find anyone. The fight had now taken up the whole of the corridor.

Cassidy traded punches with a skilful fighter. Reilly had met his match – the guy he'd kicked in the groin had recovered. Yasmine was helping Lucie to overcome another fighter. Bodie saw a knife flash at Jemma, and then the weapon ended up in the wall at her side, buried to the hilt. Like Bodie, one of Garpo's men couldn't get in on the action and was being crushed against the far door that led to the small room they'd first entered.

Behind Bodie, Heidi hauled Garpo to his feet. She was furious. She kicked him between the legs and then dragged him upright again. The man was gasping. He hung in her grasp like a rag doll.

'Please, please. Not again.'

'Then tell me what I want to know.'

Bodie left her to it, concentrating on the fight. The guy at the far end now crashed through the door and was suddenly in the tiny room, backpedalling. The fight followed him, people crabbing backwards as they fought. There was no way forwards. Bodie tried to slip past Reilly to engage in battle, but there was no way past. He would just get in the way. There had been a moment earlier where Reilly had ducked and Bodie had almost been tagged, the punch barely missing his nose.

Foot by foot, the fight moved down the corridor and then filled the little room. Bodie followed it. As he did, one of Garpo's men opened the far door and ducked out into the night. He was followed by Jemma.

The entire battle slipped outside.

CHAPTER TWENTY TWO

Among the hulking, twisted wrecks, they fought.

Bodie, at last able to get in on the action, hit a man over the head, sent him staggering, and then punched another in the throat. They were even now, and nobody had an advantage. Cassidy stood toe to toe with her opponent, both of them blocking and trading blows. Reilly took advantage of Bodie's attack on his man and pushed forward. Bodie now had his own opponent and sized him up.

Bodie fell back into a car, the metal digging hard into his spine. He reached out and threw his opponent over the bonnet of another, watching him bounce across. He followed. Around the area, men and women fought among the cars, striking them and using them to smash heads, falling across them before leaping to their feet. One of Garpo's men crashed into a tottering tower of vehicles, hitting it hard, and the whole pillar shook, then wobbled, and then came crashing down. There was the deafening sound of cars collapsing to the floor, windows smashing, metal screeching as the whole pile came down. The cars slithered away from each other under their own momentum, grinding across the ground and the gravel.

Yasmine had dived headlong to avoid the collapse and was still rolling. She came up on one knee, staring her opponent in the eye who had also rolled. Then the two launched themselves at each other.

Bodie stayed clear of the mess, though the sound rattled his teeth. His opponent had picked up a large, jagged rock and was trying to brain him with it. The guy lunged and lunged with the rock, swinging wildly but unstoppably. It was all Bodie could do to stay out of harm's way.

Reilly was sent crashing into another tower of cars. This one tottered too, the whole pile wavering. Both Reilly and his opponent scrambled away, their fight momentarily forgotten as the whole pillar swayed. It didn't fall, though, but remained unstable and unpredictable. All across the lot, the piles of cars stood in their hundreds like sentinels to the dark watches of the night, immovable.

Lucie fell across a bonnet, her spine hitting the centre. Her opponent was right in front of her. She used her momentum to kick up and out, catching him in the stomach as he leapt back. She scrambled backwards up the bonnet, trying to evade his strikes. Lucie ripped off a windscreen wiper and slashed him across the face with it, using it as a whip. The man yelped and brought his hands up, finding blood. Lucie whipped him again. He backed off warily.

Now, with more space to work, Cassidy could bring her full skill-set to the fight. She kicked and span and punched her opponent until confusion overcame him and he left himself wide open. Once he did that, the fight was over. She threw three deft punches to the throat and temples and he went down like a sack of rocks.

Bodie caught the hand that was holding the rock. He twisted it, making his opponent squeal. He turned the man around, slipped behind him, and forced him to his knees, twisting the trapped arm viciously. The man struggled, but could do nothing. He went further down. Bodie broke the arm, then came down knees first on the man's back. As he screamed, Bodie knocked him unconscious.

The melee continued throughout the scrapyard, the piles of wrecks wavering and rocking. The sound of flesh banging into metal was loud. The noise of Lucie's whip was vicious. It was a bloody, brutal, chaotic battle with no one willing to give ground.

Gradually, the relic hunters started to come out on top.

In the office, Heidi pressed Garpo to the limits. She'd already dragged him up and kicked him between the legs, and now he hung limply in her grasp. She let go of him, let him totter before her. His face was bloody, and he stood like he was already defeated.

'I won't cut you like you were gonna do to me,' she said. 'But I will change your life forever if you don't tell me what I want to know.'

'The mask,' he whispered.

'Yeah, the mask.'

'I will be killed if he finds out I told you.'

'You'll wish you were dead if you don't.'

'Please. It's more than my life's-'

Heidi had heard enough. She punched his solar plexus hard, sent him crashing and wheezing to his knees. He was crying now, crying hard.

'I *can't-*' he whimpered.

Heidi hauled him up by his throat. 'It's your balls next,' she said. 'You're gonna wish you were never born.'

She didn't want to do it, but Garpo was the next piece in the puzzle. They needed to know what he had to say.

'Please...' he said again.

'Take your chances, Garpo. They might not find out. But if you don't tell me what I want to know right now...'

Garpo stared at her, his eyes liquid. He was terrified. Heidi wondered what kind of man could instil so much fear.

'He is..he is...a...' Garpo practically sobbed. He raised both arms as if in prayer, then groaned in pain. 'Okay, okay,' he said. 'His name is Jarvis.'

Garpo hesitated, as if he'd just revealed the biggest secret of all time.

'Go on,' Heidi said.

'He...he's a courier of information. Someone who works at the top level. He knows all the criminals, all the gang leaders, all the right players. He sells information to the highest bidder, and everyone knows and respects him. He has no equal.'

'Jarvis, you say?'

'Yes, that's his name.'

'Is he well known?'

'In certain circles, yes. He's the go-to man. If you want to know something, you go to Jarvis.'

'And do you go to Jarvis?'

'He's a friend. Sometimes, we talk.'

'And you talked about the mask. Who is stealing it? When will it be stolen?'

Garpo shook his head. 'It was a brief interlude in a conversation. He mentioned the mask. I was surprised. We carried on. Nothing more.'

'All right,' Heidi shook him. 'From where does this Jarvis operate?'

Garpo looked surprised. 'From Istanbul. Have you never heard of him?'

'I'm afraid your friend's not as well known as you think, which is probably better for him. Is he on the cops' radar?'

'Jarvis helps the cops where he can. He has a free rein.'

'Sounds like he makes a lot of enemies.'

'He's very well protected. You can't even get close to him without an invitation.'

Heidi raised an eyebrow at that. 'Really? You have to be invited to talk to this guy?'

'Yes. He's very smart and cunning.'

Heidi saw it as the opposite, and an opportunity. She shook Garpo one last time. 'If you're lying to me I'll come back and decapitate you. Do you want to say anything else?'

Garpo shook his head quickly. 'No, no. It's all true. All true. Just don't tell him the information came from me. Please.'

Heidi sent Garpo into a cool oblivion, then made her way outside to help her friends. By the time she got there, they were standing around, bruised and bloody, but victorious.

Bodie stared at her. 'Did you get the info?'

Heidi nodded. 'I think we have a chance here.'

CHAPTER TWENTY THREE

Pantera answered on the second ring.

'Yeah?'

'It's me,' Bodie said. 'What do you know about an information courier who works out of Istanbul named Jarvis?'

'Oh, good morning to you, too. I'm fine, thanks.'

It actually was morning for Bodie, and he was fed, watered, and sitting in the park on a sunny day surrounded by his team. It was still relatively early, and the park was sparsely populated, giving them plenty of space to conduct their business. They had all spent a quiet night in the hotel and had risen for breakfast with the dawn.

Bodie filled Pantera in on their latest operation. 'Now,' he finished. 'We're looking for this courier of information named Jarvis.'

'Yeah, I know him. Or I know *of* him. Well respected, well protected, paranoid as fuck. You won't get close to him unless he wants you to.'

'That's what we were told,' Heidi said. 'And we want to use it.'

'How so?' Pantera sounded intrigued.

'Apparently, you have to be invited to meet with this Jarvis,' Bodie said. 'You actually need a sponsor.

We want you to get us an invite.'

'My international connections can probably make that happen. But do you think he'll just reveal his source of information?'

'That's the hope. And we're on a timer here, Jack, so don't hang around.'

Pantera ended the call without saying goodbye. Bodie looked at the other members of his team.

'Sounds like we need to start packing,' he said.

They arrived in Istanbul to a blinding hot day. The airport was crowded and noisy. They decided, since this trip was going to be different, that they wouldn't need to hire a car this time. They wouldn't be skulking around or need surveillance. At least, that was the hope. The team found a large cab and then went to a hotel, still waiting to hear back from Pantera.

By the time he called, it was getting on for the evening. The team was biding its time in the hotel bar.

Bodie answered his phone. 'Hi mate, how are you today?'

'Hilarious. I'm knackered, because I've spent the last five hours setting this up for you. No rest, no relaxation, no food. Do you know what I sacrificed for you? Beef bloody Wellington, that's what.'

'Thanks a lot, mate. It's appreciated.'

'Right. I'm supposed to be retired, do you know that? I could get into trouble if the authorities find out.'

Bodie let him get it out of his system. It didn't

take long. Pantera was just looking for attention. Bodie gave him it, thanking him again.

'Okay,' Pantera said at last when he was mollified. 'I spoke to Jarvis' managers and then I spoke to Jarvis himself. I had to tell him exactly who you were, and that you requested a sit down conversation. I had to jump through a few bloody hoops, but he's agreed to meet you.'

'Thanks, Jack,' Bodie said.

'But listen. This is you. No subterfuge, no games. Jarvis is as dangerous and smart as they come. I had to give him the truth. He knows it's the relic hunters coming to meet him, and he knows your history.'

'That's no problem,' Bodie said. 'It's what we envisioned.'

'He'll be checking up on you big time. Is there anyone who can give you negative feedback?'

Bodie thought about all the enemies they'd vanquished. 'Plenty,' he said. 'But not that he'll be able to get hold of. Some are dead, some are in jail, some are missing. I think we'll be okay.'

Pantera signed off, leaving with an appointment time and an address and words of encouragement. Bodie saw that the date was tomorrow at 2 p.m. and felt a bit deflated. He told the team.

'Looks like we have the whole day to do nothing and fret about this mask being stolen.'

But there was nothing they could do. They napped, and they showered and they ate food, and they drank water and alcohol. They wasted the day doing nothing, rested the night, and then ordered a taxi for half-past one to take them on the brief journey to Jarvis' address. It was a short drive, and soon they were standing outside in the heat, looking up at a tall white wall overhung with shrubs, and a towering black metal gate.

A guard eyed them from behind the gate.

'We have an appointment,' Bodie said.

It took a while, and they were searched twice. They also went through metal detectors and a body scanner. The guards were armed and calm and observed everything carefully. Nobody seemed rushed, and finally Bodie and his team were ushered through to their appointment.

They stood in a luxuriously appointed room with a set of bay windows to the right and a wall full of gilt-framed paintings to the left. The floor was a plush red carpet. The fixings were gold and pearl and some old bronze. There was no desk in the room, just chairs and a long couch. A low, polished coffee table separated the couch and the chairs, currently occupied with two teapots and a steaming carafe of hot black coffee.

A man rose to his feet as they entered. He was tall with long blonde hair down to his shoulders and appeared in his early fifties. His eyes were bright blue, and he instantly smiled upon seeing them.

'Oh, welcome to my home,' he said. 'The famous relic hunters. Or should that be infamous?' He laughed.

Bodie laughed with him and reached out for the proffered hand. They all shook it. 'Please, sit down,' he said. 'Tea? Coffee? Or perhaps something stronger?'

They all went for tea and coffee and soon sat back as Jarvis regaled them with a tale of Istanbul in the summer. Finally, though, Jarvis got to business.

'Well, you've come a long way,' he said. 'What can I do for you?'

'It's good of you to see us,' Bodie began. 'We are searching for information and believe you might have it.'

'It is my forte,' Jarvis said with a smile.

Bodie smiled back and took a sip of coffee before continuing. 'I won't beat about the bush here. We've been searching through America and Europe. It's come to our attention that the funerary mask of Tutankhamun in Cairo is going to be stolen. There's a heist crew being prepared and the complete plan's in place. We just need to know who's doing it and when so that we can stop it from happening.'

Bodie paused. He'd laid his cards out on the table. Honest. Open. He couldn't have said it any clearer or been more truthful. It was the right way to go with Jarvis.

Jarvis sat back and crossed his legs. He was wearing an expensive Armani suit that fit him to perfection. When he moved a gold bracelet jangled on his wrist.

'The sacred mask?' He asked. 'Of Tutankhamun. Of course. You want to prevent the theft?'

Bodie nodded. 'Our thieving days are long behind us. We help rescue relics now, save them from tyrants and bring them into the light for everyone to see. We're on the good side now.' He smiled.

Jarvis nodded. 'I see. That's an interesting idea, you trying to stop a theft. I like it. And I may have some information.'

Bodie leaned forward. 'Which is?'

'Oh, it will not be that easy, my friend. You know what I am? I am a trader. I trade information between people, between organisations. It's my job, my gift. If you want information, you must give me something in return.'

Bodie wasn't sure of his position and frowned. 'What do you mean?'

'I can give you information. I can trade it. What do you have to trade for it?'

Bodie didn't want to say *'nothing'*. He frowned. 'What do you want?'

Jarvis snapped his fingers. 'Now, that's the attitude. You say your stealing days are in your past?'

Bodie's eyes narrowed. 'You want us to do something for you?'

Jarvis nodded. 'You help me, I help you. That's how I deal.'

Bodie sighed. 'What do you want from us?'

Jarvis looked pleased. He put his teacup down, rose and walked over to the window. He looked out for a while.

'I want you to steal something important,' he said.

CHAPTER TWENTY FOUR

Their target was a brand new office building in the middle of Istanbul. Inside, there was a safe and, inside that, was a folder of documents that concealed lots of vital information. Jarvis wanted the information. In his own words, it was worth more than gold.

The relic hunters wasted no time. They drove to the building in question, checked out the interior and the various offices, pretending to be customers looking for someone who clearly wasn't there. They studied everything they could see without arousing suspicion. The offices were guarded by a security team that occupied the lobby and probably did several walk-throughs per night. The office they were targeting was on the second floor. Whilst Bodie and Jemma did a recce of the inside, the rest of the team patrolled the outside and looked for weak spots.

Hours later, they met back at the car, armed with information.

'What do we have?' Bodie asked.

They shared everything. It wasn't long before they had a plan. During their walkthrough, Bodie had noticed that the windows weren't wired. He had to assume that the guards did a nightly walk around so the rooms wouldn't have sensors, either. That was the payoff for having security. You couldn't activate a sensor except in closed off rooms.

The building was low key, out of the way. Bodie, Cassidy and Jemma, the best of the thieves, were going in. Midnight passed, and all was still. Soon, they were ready to go.

The building blazed against the night, its lobby in full illumination. The offices on the top three floors stood in darkness. Bodie could see one guard sitting at a desk through the windows of the lobby.

He moved through the warm dark, stealthy and quiet. He crossed a path and then a large patch of grass and then hid among bushes. Cassidy and Jemma were at his side. They didn't need words; each confidently knew what the other was going to do.

Bodie raced to the side of the building, reached up, and started cutting the window. He worked quickly and professionally, cutting a gap his hand would fit through. When he was done, he used a suction cup to pull the cut glass free so that it wouldn't fall into the room and make a noise. He placed the circle carefully on the floor, then reached through the new gap and undid the window.

It slid open. The team waited, listening to the inside and outside. Nothing moved, nothing had changed. Bodie hefted himself up first, crossing the window ledge and coming down inside the building. Cassidy followed and then Jemma, each as fleet as the one before, each as covert.

Jemma closed the window. Bodie remembered the layout from their recce before. He went to the back of the office and peered through a vision panel. Nobody was around. Bodie eased open the door and went through into a darkened hallway. He wasted no time dashing to its far end where another door stood, this one wedged open. Again, he looked through it and beyond. He couldn't see anything, couldn't hear anything. He thought maybe they employed only one night guard.

He went through the door and then found the stairs. They were concrete and shouldn't make any sound. He motioned to Cassidy and Jemma and then started up, a riser at a time, taking it steady.

Up to the first floor they went. It was as they stepped onto the first floor landing that Bodie heard a noise from below. He crouched, peering through some spindles at the floor below. A figure passed by as if heading for the stairs and he readied himself to move fast. But the figure passed the stairs by and continued into a nearby restroom. It was the same guard who'd been stationed in the lobby.

'Keep going,' Cassidy whispered.

Bodie was already on it. He turned, found the right hallway, and then started along it. He stayed low, beneath the windows, just in case someone was actually in here working in the dark. Weirder things had happened. He passed three doors, and then came to the one they wanted. The number on the door read 212.

Bodie pushed it open. Together, the three of them went inside and got a feel for the place. It was wide and full of partitioned-off desks. There was a door in the far wall, and it was towards this that Bodie stalked.

He reached it quickly and pushed it open. This would be the manager's office. It contained a small desk and two chairs and was nicely furnished. The owner clearly felt at home here. Bodie saw the safe right away.

It was sitting on the floor in the far corner, a five foot high steel box that contained the secrets Bodie needed. He walked straight over to it and crouched down in front of it.

'Here we go,' he whispered.

Jemma was the best safecracker of them all. She bent down now and, in absolute silence, put her ear to the steel door and started turning the wheel. Bodie could only sit back and watch and stay still. Cassidy went to the outer door and checked the hallway. For now, they were safe.

Jemma worked steadily and slowly, head bent to the front of the safe. She stopped every so often, listening hard. Her facial expression never changed; sheer concentration.

Bodie waited patiently. Right then, Cassidy reappeared at the door and gave them a warning sign. The guard was making his patrol. Jemma shook her head. She couldn't stop her work. She ignored Cassidy and Bodie and kept on working.

The guard came into the outer office. Bodie stayed where he was, hoping he'd leave it at that, hoping he wouldn't venture into the interior office. Cassidy stayed on one side of the door, waiting.

Footsteps came towards them. Bodie shook his head. This would not go well. He wanted to ask Jemma if she was nearly done, but knew he couldn't interrupt her. The footsteps came closer. Cassidy prepared herself.

The door opened. The guard's figure appeared. He stayed outside, staring at Bodie. He didn't look surprised to see him standing there.

'Don't be scared,' Bodie said. 'We're not here to hurt you.'

The guard aimed his torch around the room, saw Jemma, and now Cassidy stepped out into the light. The guard bit his bottom lip and the torchlight shook a little.

'What do you want?' he asked.

Bodie pointed at the safe. 'Nothing much. Just some information. We're nearly there.'

The guard clearly felt threatened. He wasn't armed. He stared at all three of them as if trying to gauge what his reaction should be. Cassidy was close enough to grab him if he tried to run.

'I can't let you do that,' the man said.

Bodie didn't want to strong-arm him. 'Please,' he said. 'This doesn't have to go bad. We're not bad people. We've been forced into this.'

'Forced?'

'Yeah, by a bad guy. We're not the criminals here.'

'From where I'm standing, that's exactly what you are.'

Bodie didn't want to hurt this guy. Cassidy was ready, just waiting for his signal. They could grab him, knock him out, tie him up. But Bodie had had enough of violence for one week.

He reached slowly into his pockets, not wanting to harm the man. 'How about this?' he said. He opened his wallet and counted out some notes. Jemma made a delighted sound, then reached for the safe's handle and twisted it. The safe cracked open. Jemma looked up at Bodie expectantly.

Bodie waved the cash. 'Five hundred dollars,' he said. 'To look the other way.'

The guard licked his lips, eyes on the money. 'Are you serious?'

Bodie nodded. 'Deadly. You can have the money if you let us walk away.'

The guard swallowed heavily, trying to decide which way to jump. A heavy tension filled the room.

'Let us help you,' Bodie said softly.

The guard seemed to come to a decision. He stepped into the room, passed Cassidy with a wary glance, and came right up to Bodie. He took the money and stuffed it into his trousers. Then he gave Bodie a wry look.

'You know what's gonna have to happen?' Bodie asked.

The guard nodded. 'Yeah. Someone's gonna have to hit me and tie me up.'

'That'll be me,' Cassidy said eagerly.

'Don't leave too much of a mark,' the guard said.

Meanwhile, Jemma was searching inside the safe. She found a folder just like the one Jarvis had described and held it up.

'Pay dirt,' she said.

Bodie looked at Cassidy. 'Leave a mark,' he said. 'But don't make it too bad.'

CHAPTER TWENTY FIVE

Jarvis was still up and waiting for them when they returned to his house. He had changed into an all white suit, slippers, and a jaunty hat that he wore at an angle. He had seven tumblers of bourbon lined up on their side of the desk and waved at them as the relic hunters walked in.

'To a job well done,' he said. 'I assume it was well done?'

Jemma waved the folder at him. 'We have everything you asked for.'

'I hope you haven't read it.'

'Not our style,' Bodie said. 'You know what we want in return.'

Jarvis picked up his own tumbler and held it high in the air. 'To you,' he said. 'The famed relic hunters proving they've still got it.'

Bodie didn't want to think that they'd broken the law tonight, that they had indeed gone back to their 'old ways'. It was a hard moral dilemma, and he didn't want to face it. Not tonight, not really ever.

'Don't worry,' Jarvis said, as if reading his mind. 'You stole off criminals. And it's nothing dangerous. Just a ledger detailing how their organisation works. The information will be helpful to me.'

Bodie took his tumbler and found a chair. The bourbon was good. The team sat down and watched as Jarvis paced up and down behind his desk.

'Okay, now it's my turn,' the man said. 'The funerary mask of Tutankhamun. The heist is close, very close. I have two sources of information, and both whisper that the theft is imminent. You will have to hurry. Maybe you are already too late,' he shrugged. 'I can't help that. But you know where it is, and you know the theft is happening soon.'

'Who is stealing it?' Bodie asked.

Jarvis stopped his pacing and turned to them. 'A very dangerous man named the Salamander has commissioned the entire operation. Have you heard of him?'

Bodie blinked. He recalled the name. 'Recently,' he said. 'Isn't he some kind of criminal private collector? Something like that.'

'He's a hell of a lot more than that,' Jarvis said. 'The Salamander is a notorious, untouchable criminal. Sly and clever. Known to the international police community and yet too shady to prosecute. They haven't been able to pin anything on him in all his years and the more they try, the worse it gets for them. Loss of face. Sackings. Demotions. He always comes out on top. It's expected that he has numerous works of art squirrelled away somewhere and has paid for many of them to be stolen. The funerary mask is the latest in a long line, I'm afraid.'

'Where can we find him?' Heidi asked.

'Oh, that I cannot tell you for even I do not know. In any case, I would not want to be on his wrong side. He is vicious.'

'The Salamander won't be stealing the mask himself,' Jemma said. 'He must have hired a team.'

'And there's your other piece of information. I can tell you he's hired a team very much like yourselves. A professional outfit tasked with stealing the mask. You will be going up against yourselves,' Jarvis laughed.

Bodie didn't. He sipped the bourbon. 'Names?'

'None, I'm afraid. I do not know the team that he's hired. I can, however, give you a couple of my contacts in Cairo. Just mention my name and they will help you.' He reeled off a couple of names and contact numbers. 'And that,' he said pleasantly. 'Makes us even. Do you think?'

Jemma tapped the folder and placed it gently on the desk. She sat back, sipping her drink. Jarvis made no move for the folder.

'Our business has concluded,' Bodie put the tumbler back on the desk. 'Thanks for the drink.'

'What will you do now?' Jarvis asked.

Bodie glanced at the team. 'We have no choice,' he said. 'But to go to Cairo. We'll talk to your contacts there.'

'It's been a long road here,' Reilly said. 'We should have known it would end up with the Salamander.'

'Few have heard of him outside the usual circles,' Jarvis said. 'He's a slippery one.'

'Do you know where he lives?' Cassidy asked.

'Even I don't know everything,' Jarvis shrugged. 'It's important I stay in my lane. If I stray to either side, I will attract the wrong attention. And I don't need to be knowing where the Salamander lives.'

Bodie nodded and leaned forward, even more

conscious now of the tight deadline. Jarvis had told them that the theft was near. They had to get to Cairo and try to thwart it as soon as they possibly could. He rose to his feet.

'It's been...unreal,' he said. He hadn't enjoyed doing business with Jarvis, but it had been an experience. The whole team finished their drinks and rose and said their goodbyes. Jarvis nodded at all of them.

Bodie went to the door, his mind already focused on Cairo. Lucie, he saw, had her phone out and was probably looking up flights. They would need to hop on the earliest plane possible.

'How are we going to stop the theft of a sacred item without alerting the authorities?' Cassidy asked quietly.

'The best way we can,' Bodie replied.

They hurried out into the night.

CHAPTER TWENTY SIX

Cairo was hot and dusty and hectic. It started at the airport and never let up. It was a dry, sultry day, and it hit the team right in the face as they left the airport.

So did the noise. Cairo was manic, non-stop. The team decided not to hire a car and took a taxi to their hotel in which they quickly unpacked. Ten minutes later, they were down in the lobby, trying to decide what to do first.

Even the lobby was packed with people. It was difficult to hear each other. Bodie found a quiet corner at the back, next to some potted plants. He waited for the others to crowd around.

'My thoughts,' he said. 'We contact Jarvis' people. See if they have anything new. Let's start there.'

The team agreed. Heidi put in the call to the first and dropped Jarvis' name. The man answered on the first ring.

'Mo here.' The voice spoke in Egyptian Arabic.

'Hi Mo. My name's Heidi. Jarvis told me I could speak to you.'

The voice grew wary and switched to decent English. 'He did? Okay then. What do you want to know?'

The Sacred Mask

Expecting a request for information straight away. Heidi licked her lips. 'We're here regarding the funerary mask. The one in the Egyptian Museum right here in Cairo. We know a team is planning to steal it. Do you have any more information?'

Mo was silent for a while. Finally, he spoke up. 'All I know is what Malik told me. That a team plans to steal it for the Salamander. I do not know when. You should talk to Malik. He is closer to the Salamander's contacts than I am.'

Malik was the other name Jarvis had given them. Heidi thanked Mo for his time and searched for the other number. When she found it, she placed the call. Malik answered on the third ring and Heidi went through the same speech.

'Oh, yes, the mask,' Malik said. 'Yes, yes, the chatter has really ramped up on that in the last few days. They're gonna have to be careful so the authorities don't get wind of it. I heard something just this morning.' He stopped.

'Which was...' Heidi prompted.

'Oh, yes, yes, that the mask job is going down tonight.'

Heidi frowned. Just like that. Tonight.

'Are you sure?'

'That's the word I'm getting. Are you guys wanting to steal it first?'

'No, nothing like that. Did you hear anything else?'

'Just stuff about the crack team that's gonna steal it. Ex special forces apparently that turned their hands to thieving. They're world class. Used to do this kind of thing for their country. Very hush hush.

There's six of them, and they do like a bit of combat.'

'Not tonight they won't,' Heidi said. 'The jobs gotta be done quietly and they're under contract with the Salamander.'

'Yes, yes, tonight will be different. They will be in and out like ghosts.'

'It's a big job,' Heidi said. 'Any idea how they plan to pull it off?'

Marko sighed. 'No, my abilities do not go that far, I'm afraid. Only the inner circle will know that.'

Heidi thanked him for his time and hung up. She stared at the team. 'Fuck,' she said. 'It's happening tonight.'

They had overheard. Now Bodie checked the time. 'It's only ten o'clock,' he said. 'We have time to prepare.'

'Prepare what?' Yasmine asked.

'Prepare how we're gonna stop this,' Bodie said.

They got their heads together in a quiet place and made a plan. They went out to buy everything they needed, including backpacks and torches and water, and they bought dark clothing and even darker masks. It was a fraught few hours but, when they all met in Bodie and Heidi's hotel room, they were ready to act.

It was two p.m.

'We still have plenty of time,' Bodie said. 'What time does the museum close?'

'Six,' Lucie said.

'So we go in before six and we find a place to hide,' Bodie said. 'That gives us a long wait until the thieves arrive. Wherever we hide, it's gonna have to be good.'

But he had faith in them. They were good at their

respective jobs. He looked at them, all dressed in dark clothing with their backpacks ready and faces set for battle. They were all up for saving the funerary mask of Tutankhamun.

'This has been one of the oddest ops ever,' Bodie said. 'But I'm glad we can finally see it out. I know that going into the museum is risking our necks, too. But I can't see any other way to do this. When the other team arrives, we're gonna be waiting.'

They all nodded. They decided to grab a large meal since they wouldn't be eating again that day and headed down to the restaurant. It was as busy as everywhere else, and they were forced to wait half an hour for a table. Still, they had time.

Bodie ate steak and drank water and took his time. The restaurant was so noisy they couldn't hear each other speak. It was packed too. They were almost rubbing elbows with the next table.

When five o'clock came around, the team left the restaurant and grabbed a taxi to the Egyptian Museum. The car fought its way through the evening traffic. Bodie imagined this was rush hour, but the traffic always seemed the same. Crazy. It wasn't far. In fact, Bodie thought, they could probably have walked it almost as fast.

The driver dropped them off close to the museum. It was a grand edifice that stretched left to right from an archway and an open door. Three flags topped the roof. There was an ornamental garden out front and palm trees and small sphinxes. And, of course, droves of people.

Bodie sweated in the dry heat. He shrugged his backpack on and started walking towards the front door. It was a simple walk made hard by the amount of people milling around. Many were just standing and talking in the majesty of the giant construction. Some were filing out, others making their way inside. Bodie and his team walked up to the front doors.

Inside, they grabbed a pocket guide and found out where the funerary mask was being displayed. It was five-forty-five. An announcement came over the loudspeaker system that the museum would close in fifteen minutes. People looked disappointed. Some made their way towards the exit. Other headed deeper into the museum, determined to wring every drop from their visit. The further they were inside, the longer it would take to get them out.

'This way,' Lucie said, having commandeered the guide book.

They followed her through several rooms of Egyptian statues and weapons and Canopic jars. They took their time, only paying attention when they were getting close to the mask. Bodie saw it first, a resplendent, ancient, colourful work of art standing behind a glass cabinet in pride of place.

'Wow,' he said. 'If I were still a thief, I'd wanna steal it too.'

Lucie shook her head. 'Let's keep that quiet, eh? It's beautiful.'

'So where the hell are we gonna hide?' Cassidy said.

They were cutting it fine. Soon, the museums people would start sweeping out the guests. In eight minutes, to be precise.

Bodie and the others agreed to split up and meet back at the mask in five minutes. Bodie went straight and found himself headed down two flights of stairs into a large room with high ceilings and walls. It was supposed to look airy and huge, and maybe even a little intimidating, but Bodie wasn't really paying attention to that.

He was looking for a place to hide.

He searched and searched. Despite this place being massive, everything was well spread out and standing on its own, as if inviting attention. Bodie saw nowhere to hide. He paid attention to the walls too, looking for niches or doors or anything that might offer the slightest possibility but, in five minutes, he was back at the mask.

'Nothing,' he said. 'I hope you've done better than me.'

Most of the others shook their heads. It was Lucie who gave them a smile.

'I think I've found something,' she said. 'A janitor's room. It's locked, which is good. If we can pick the lock, get inside, and then lock it again, the museum guards and curators have no reason to suspect anyone's inside. And it's just a few seconds walk from the mask.'

Bodie grinned. He liked it. Quickly, they followed Lucie to the door in question and then stood around it as if talking. Jemma bent to the task. In about eighteen seconds, she had the door unlocked.

The team filed quickly into the janitor's room. Bodie was last, making sure nobody saw them going inside. He closed the door, and then Jemma once again took her picks out and started on the lock. This time, she locked it and stood up.

'Job done,' she said.

Now they had to wait. It was six o'clock. They had no idea when the thieves were going to turn up.

Bodie hunkered down to wait.

CHAPTER TWENTY SEVEN

Time passed slowly in the cramped space.

The seven of them made themselves as comfortable as possible, and tried not to keep checking the time. Nothing would happen until at least midnight, and probably later. It was a slow, confined wait, made harder because none of them could talk.

About eight o'clock someone tried the door. Bodie and the others tensed. They stared at the handle, saw it turning twice more. Bodie prayed not to hear the key rattling in the lock.

His prayer seemed to work. Outside, the security guard outside must have been satisfied because nothing else happened. The knob rattled again at ten o'clock and, again, all was well. The guards were used to certain locked doors. Bodie made a note that the guard appeared once every two hours, on the nose of the hour.

Midnight came close, the seconds passing like hours. Soon, one of them would have to reconnoitre the area and start keeping an eye out for the thieves. He wondered how it would happen. He expected something high tech, something that knocked out the cameras and the sensors and everything else, and then a covert entry. He expected guards, if they appeared, to be treated severely. That was how this team would work. They would take no chances.

'Who's gonna take watch outside?' he whispered at midnight.

'I'll do it,' Jemma said. 'I'm the cat burglar.'

Bodie nodded. She was the best bet. She was quick and quiet and stealthy, probably more so than he. Jemma rose to her feet and approached the door. She opened it, looked out, and then paused.

'Guard in the hall,' she said. 'Walking around.'

She waited. Soon, she exited the little room and disappeared. Bodie stood with the others, hoping she would be okay.

In the hall, Jemma crept from display cabinet to display cabinet. She stayed low and quiet. The hall was silent as the grave. It felt a little spooky in the dead of night, being surrounded by all these relics under the stark light. She wished the team had a comms system set up, where she could communicate with them, but this mission was purely on a shoestring. It had been cobbled together on the fly and they'd had no time to plan.

She crouched in the dark, her eyes on the mask.

Back in the room, Bodie set about relocking the door. They couldn't leave anything to chance.

Cassidy whispered, 'What are we gonna do with these guys after we neutralise them?'

'Leave 'em for the guards to find,' Reilly said with a smile.

Bodie raised an eyebrow. 'You know, that's not a bad idea. It'll save us having to explain our presence.'

'Also something that's been bothering me,' Heidi

said. 'We look as guilty as the thieves at the moment.'

'We should have no problem stealing out of here,' Bodie said. 'Trust us.'

'We're also trusting in the skills of our enemies,' Lucie said. 'Trusting they're gonna get in here at the right time when no guards are around. That's a big one for me.'

Bodie shrugged. 'We must assume they're competent. They have a big rep. And the Salamander wouldn't have commissioned a set of dummies.'

They were silent for a while. Bodie wondered how Jemma was doing out there alone. Time slipped by. It was half-past twelve.

It was two thirty a.m. when there came a soft knock on the door. That would be Jemma. Bodie looked around.

'This is it.'

He unlocked the door and looked out into Jemma's face. She said, 'They're here,' and moved away. Bodie followed her, staying silent and low. One by one, the relic hunters slid out of the room and into the hall. They crept around two exhibits to where they could easily see the funerary mask.

Bodie watched carefully. He could see the six thieves, all clad in black and wearing masks, slinking through shadows in the far corner of the room. They had arrived through the ducts, perhaps after negating any alarm sensors that may exist. Bodie saw a tall, rail thin man and a broad chested guy. He saw a squat, powerful man as they came closer. They skulked from exhibit to exhibit, approaching the mask.

Bodie watched them work. They came as a fluid

team, working together, each one functioning independently but staying together as a whole. They were good. Steadily, the leader approached the cabinet that housed the funerary mask.

He stopped before it.

At that moment, Bodie heard footsteps. A guard was approaching. His own team crouched as low as they could go, hiding as best they could. The new team slinked away into whatever shadows they could find.

The guard entered the hall, sauntering along. He checked nothing carefully. Through procrastination and weariness, he gave everything a cursory glance. He patted the top of his leg as he walked and chewed his gums.

The black-clad team let him get close. Then, pouncing fast, one of them came up behind the guy, looped an arm around his throat, and jerked him off his feet.

Bodie swallowed. He'd hoped they'd let the guard go, but they weren't taking the risk. The man choked the guard until he passed out and then let him slip to the floor. Quickly, they tethered and gagged him.

The apparent leader then gestured sharply at the mask, as if telling his team to get a move on. The team crowded around the cabinet as one man used a handcrafted tool to open the glass door. He took his time, despite the leader's impatience. Bodie hoped to God no alarms would go off. If they did, they were all screwed.

But the team was good. They opened the display cabinet, edged the mask away from its moorings, and appeared to be paying attention to a pressure switch.

Bodie let them work. Of course, he assumed they'd neutralised any cameras that might be focused on the room. That was an assumption right from the start. How else could they steal the mask?

He didn't want them to get too far along, but he took a while to study them. The leader was impatient and taut; the others stood around with little professionalism, and nobody had been left as lookout or to watch over the downed guard. One man worked hard whilst the others watched.

The leader urged more speed. The man holding the mask didn't respond, just concentrated on his work. The fallen guard was still unconscious, though his radio made a sudden crackle that made everyone jump.

But it was just a crackle. Nobody was trying to get hold of him, it seemed. Bodie assumed he was overdue to report in somewhere, but maybe they didn't do it that way in this museum. Maybe he just made a round every hour and returned to his station.

Bodie turned to the others. 'Brace yourselves. This could get hairy.'

Cassidy smiled. 'I'm ready for that.'

Lucie nodded. 'There are seven of us to their six.'

'But they're special forces,' Reilly said. 'Different beast.'

'We're pretty special ourselves,' Bodie said. 'Now, stay with me.'

The team stepped head-first into the confrontation.

CHAPTER TWENTY EIGHT

Bodie stepped out of concealment and started walking towards the black-clad team.

'Hey, man,' he said, his voice pitched so just they could hear it. 'You need to put the mask back.'

The other team all started. The masks all turned towards Bodie and he heard a cry of astonishment. It was a bit unnerving, staring at six faceless people, seeing no facial expressions, but he forged on with his own team at his back.

'We're here to stop you stealing the mask,' he said.

The leader didn't move a muscle. The one stealing the mask made a quick decision and put it back for now. He turned towards Bodie.

'Who the hell are you?' He spoke with a British accent.

'Guardians of the mask,' Bodie said with a grin. 'We've tracked you all the way from America.'

'Your mistake,' the leader said, his mouth moving under the tight material. 'Walk away. We don't want to kill you tonight.'

Bodie had noticed that the other team carried no weapons. They had wanted to move lightly and swiftly and unencumbered, and to rely on their own skills.

'Nobody wants a fight in here,' the leader said. 'We'll all get caught.'

'Is that you surrendering?' Bodie asked, stopping about eight feet away from the man.

The black-clad team moved forward as one now until they flanked their leader. Now, they looked like a unit.

'This isn't the place for this,' the leader sounded pissed and unhappy.

Bodie spread his hands. 'We're not going anywhere. So now you give up.'

'You really think that's gonna happen?' the man now sounded annoyed.

'We need to get a move on,' the man beside him said.

Bodie smiled. 'We have all the time in the world.'

The leader crossed his arms. 'How about you switch to our side?' he said. 'There's a lot of wonga involved and some of it could be yours.'

'We're not in it for the money,' Bodie said.

'Well, what are you in it for?'

'The relic. The museum, and the people who come here every day. For justice, and what's right. Why should an asshole like the Salamander be arrogant enough to believe he deserves to *own* a sacred treasure?'

The leader shrugged. 'I just work for the money. Some of it could be yours. And you'd get a big rep for pulling off a job like this.'

Bodie shook his head. 'Not for us.'

The leader moved his head. 'That go for all of you?' he asked. 'Or do some of you want to switch sides?'

Bodie laughed. 'You won't get any joy there, pal.'

Now the leader spread his arms as if he was resigned. 'Then it looks like we're gonna have to kill you.'

The man lunged forward, the rest of his team moving at exactly the same time as if synced. It caught Bodie by surprise, seeing all of them move like that. He should have been ready, but he wasn't.

He stepped back, then felt the presence of his team at his sides. They were ready. And now they all leapt forward, meeting the attack.

Both teams crashed together with an audible, meaty thump. Fists flew. Bodie met the team leader, pretended to throw a haymaker, and then jabbed in with a deft jab to the throat. The leader ducked away and came back with several hits of his own, all of which Bodie blocked. The man stepped in and tried to grab hold of Bodie, tried to throw him, but Bodie leapt away, now circling.

Cassidy met her opponent with a crunch, neither of them giving way. They bounced off each other. Cassidy then threw a series of punches that forced the man back, sent him rebounding off a display cabinet. He couldn't move fast enough to retaliate. It was all defence. Even with the mask on, his body language showed total surprise.

It was both unnerving and spooky to be fighting these mask-wearing men. Bodie was used to seeing facial expressions, to seeing pain and shock and arrogance. The faceless men were intimidating in more ways than one.

Bodie was in the centre of the melee. Through the hall, the fight spread out. Everyone stepped lightly and tried to make as little noise as possible, and now Bodie felt relief that their guard was already negated.

Reilly barrelled into his own opponent, striking him in the chest and forcing him back. He came up under the man's chin head first and knocked him to his knees. Reilly moved in for a quick takedown, but the man was tough and rolled away, coming up faster than Reilly could believe, already poised for another attack. Reilly didn't hold back. He rushed in, jabbing his fists in front of him. It was a mistake. The other guy was ready. He blocked and then sidestepped and then jabbed stiffened fingers into Reilly's ribs.

Pain exploded in his side.

Reilly tried to cover up and slink away. The man wouldn't let him. He pursued his advantage, punching at Reilly's head and body.

Heidi grabbed her enemy and tried to throw him. The man was caught by surprise. He went flying through the air and came down on his back, landing on his spine. He grunted through the mask. Heidi straddled him, raining blows down on his exposed head and throat. He blocked her several times, but the blows started to get through. He tried to buck her off. Heidi clamped hard with her thighs. She wasn't going anywhere.

Lucie and Jemma took another man, coming in from left and right. He fought them off at first, but they kept coming, dancing away and then striking back, hitting precisely and with speed. He couldn't look both ways at once though, and started to take damage. Lucie and Jemma stayed at it.

Yasmine had her own opponent, and slid across the floor so she hit him at crotch height. This was done on purpose, and it staggered the man. He didn't fall to his knees, but he doubled up. Yasmine punched upwards into his face, into the centre of the mask. She heard a deep groan. She punched at the nose and the eyes and the ears. He stayed doubled over, still recovering. When he did stand upright once more, Yasmine again jabbed out at his groin, catching him a solid blow. The man was in hell.

Bodie and the leader were at a stalemate. They both attacked and blocked equally well, and it appeared to be coming down to stamina. The leader, though, was in a hurry. His movements were rushed, and twice he almost made a mistake in haste. All Bodie needed was one. He circled the man now, drawing it out, trying to make him anxious. Bodie took his time. The other man couldn't.

The noise in the hall was relatively, surprisingly tame. Nobody spoke. The only sound was gasping and groaning, and their feet were muffled by their boots. Only once did someone crash into a display case and rattle the glass. Someone cursed when it happened, but the noise didn't carry too far.

Bodie stayed away from the leader, bating the man. He was ready for an attack, and it soon came. The leader stepped in, swivelled, and tried a spinning kick. Bodie saw it coming a mile off and raised an arm to block it. At the same time, he jabbed with his left, striking the man's ribs and making him gasp. The leader buckled.

But the black-clad team was tough. They took the blows and recovered. They kept coming, never letting up. Jemma and Lucie were close to beating their opponent, still darting in from both sides. Heidi was still on top of hers, beating him mercilessly. His movements were slowing.

Cassidy never let up. She was tireless, smashing blows against her opponent. He could do nothing but defend and was probably one large bruise. But Cassidy forced him back and back until he could go no further. He came up against a wall and she held him there, launching attack after attack.

Bodie ducked as the leader threw a double punch. He almost ducked right into a rising knee, but saw it at the last moment and managed to force his head aside. The knee brushed his ear. Bodie continued to the ground and then used the floor's shiny surface to help him swivel right around. His legs, moving at speed, caught the leader and took him off his feet. The man crashed to the floor, grunting in shock.

Bodie leapt at him, trying to press the advantage. The leader brought his arms up. Bodie punched into his ribs, smashing as hard as he could. The man covered up, but not in time, still taking a couple of solid blows. Bodie climbed on top of him.

Throughout the great hall, the battle continued. There were groans and grunts and small cries of pain, the sound of boots and knees striking flesh and bone. Through light and shadow the embattled figures fought each other as soundlessly as possible, the masks unnerving, the whole spectacle out of the ordinary.

The relic hunters were winning.

CHAPTER TWENTY NINE

Jemma and Lucie felled their man and then punched him until he stopped moving. Cassidy smashed her way through her opponent's defences, then smashed his sternum, his ribs, and his face. He slithered to his knees before her. Yasmine hurt the thief before her until he squirmed in pain. Reilly broke one of his enemy's fingers and then elbowed him in the jaw, hearing an audible snap. Heidi was tiring atop her adversary, but she still threw her punches and now he was tiring even more. His defence was crumbling.

Bodie was thrown off his man and rolled into an upright position. The leader didn't follow him right away, though. He was hurt. The man cradled his ribs and then climbed painfully to his feet. Bodie took a small breather. Yes, he knew he should push for the advantage, but this was one of the hardest fights he'd ever had, and he was breathing heavily and bruised.

He glanced around the room. The black-clad team appeared to be the worst off. The leader looked too, and then he broke protocol.

'Run!' he yelled. 'Plan B. Do it now.'

Bodie was shocked. The leader started running towards the hall's exit, and then so did the entirety of his team. They broke away from their various skirmishes and followed the man across the floor towards the far doors.

Bodie checked that the funerary mask was still there, and then took off in pursuit. Again, he was assuming that, if this was Plan B, then the enemy must have prepared for it. If they followed them directly, they'd be part of the same plan.

Whatever that may be.

The relic hunters chased the black-clad team. They ran through the great hall, bypassing exhibits and trying not to slip on the polished floor. Bodie saw cameras mounted up high, but assumed the other team had dealt with them. No alarms were being raised, nobody came running. Ahead, the thieves were arrowing through the halls, running as a group without looking back.

Bodie and his team stayed with them. They were ten yards behind, then a little further as the thieves sped up. Bodie increased his speed too, hoping to catch them. He was bleeding and bruised, but determined. The air rushed past his face. He chanced a quick look around and saw his team all with the same dogged looks on their faces.

They flew through the halls. The lead team increased their pace. Bodie was sweating hard. He passed sphinxes and dozens of statues. He passed paintings and display cabinets and platforms. It was a hard run. Bodie couldn't run any faster and he was losing the race.

The thieves seemed to be following a particular pattern through each hall and were running to one side. They'd clearly mapped this route beforehand and were sticking to it. They were still running as a group, well-disciplined.

Cassidy came up to Bodie's side. 'We're not gonna catch them,' she panted. 'They're too fast.'

'I thought that too,' he said.

'We foiled the robbery,' she said. 'We did it.'

'My thoughts exactly,' he said. 'But we can't stop chasing them now. Clearly, they planned this route and took measures to escape detection. We have to follow them out.'

Cassidy cursed. 'Hadn't thought of that.'

They stayed on the tail of the thieves, running as fast as they could. Lucie was panting hard and falling behind a little. Bodie couldn't slow. He had to hope she stayed with them. There couldn't be much further to go.

They pounded up a series of steps, came to another hall, and ran around the far side. They flew past a row of windows. Bodie was labouring.

Ahead now, the team slowed. The leader glanced back, saw they were being followed, and turned away. He grabbed for a side door, flung it open, and raced out into the night. When he did so, the building's alarms activated.

'Shit,' Bodie said.

The thieves ran out of the door, flowing outside. Bodie and his team were there a dozen seconds later, and used the same door. Already, they could hear loud sirens in the air. Bodie found himself in a grand plaza with more statues and sphinxes. He dashed after the thieves, finding they were headed for the back of the museum and the maze of twisty streets that lay there.

The thieves were even further ahead.

'We're not gonna catch them,' Bodie yelled. 'Let's make sure of our own safety.'

'We did it,' Heidi was yelling back. 'We saved the mask.'

Bodie was happy about it, but first they had to make sure they didn't get caught. A look back at the door told him there were no guards around yet. Ahead, the thieves had vanished.

Bodie slowed and let his team catch up. They raced through the dark, under dim lights, now running blind. They did not know where they were or where they were going. The building ended, and they were in the street. It was late. Bodie saw a few other people wandering and a group of youths. He wasn't running anymore.

Sirens approached the museum.

Bodie melted away with his team, threading the unfamiliar streets.

CHAPTER THIRTY

The next morning Bodie overslept. He meant to. He was in a happy place. They had started this mission with barely nothing, but had managed to track the thieves across two continents on little but breadcrumbs. They had started out wanting to foil the robbery of Tutankhamun's funerary mask, and they had done exactly that.

Bodie was feeling very pleased with himself.

When he woke, Heidi was still sleeping. He didn't wake her, but messaged the group chat to see if anyone was down at breakfast. Both Cassidy and Lucie were. Bodie joined them and grinned. He saluted with a mug of hot black coffee.

'Here's to success,' he said.

They saluted back. They were all smiling. Bodie went up to the buffet and grabbed himself a full English breakfast. When he sat back down, they were still smiling.

'The museum knows it's a target now,' he said. 'It knows the funerary mask is the objective because it was tampered with. That guard is okay. What more could we ask for?'

'I guess we could phone in an anonymous tip,' Lucie said. 'Tell the cops who's responsible. Everything we know.'

'The Salamander will be livid,' Cassidy said. 'He might even try again.'

'At least this time the museum will be prepared properly for it,' Bodie said. 'We can't do more than what we've done.'

One by one, the others joined them. Bodie ate his meal slowly and then refilled his coffee cup. It was a pleasant morning that stretched into a happy afternoon. They retired to the lobby and sprawled out there where it was the least noisy. The team was aching, cut and bruised, but content.

Bodie had no plans, no direction, and it was nice for a little while. They didn't have to return to New York yet.

'We should start looking at flights,' Lucie said right at that moment, making him smile. 'What is it?'

'I was just thinking we don't have to return right away,' he said. 'I was thinking it's nice not to have responsibilities for a while.'

Lucie put away her phone. 'Good point. We could stay here a few nights.'

'Check out the pyramids,' Cassidy said. 'See what trouble we can get ourselves into.'

'You never know,' Reilly said. 'We might find a relic they've overlooked. It is what we do.'

Bodie enjoyed the peace of the moment. He should have known it wouldn't last. The team ordered a round of drinks despite the hour of the day and settled back for a long afternoon of rest and relaxation. It had been a tough week chasing down the Salamander's cronies. Now they deserved a brief respite.

Bodie chatted to Heidi for a while. The couple

were enjoying their relatively new relationship. It had been a long time coming, but inevitable. At least, that was what the others said. Inevitable. Bodie wasn't sure he liked the sound of that.

The afternoon passed like a slow-moving river. It was good. Bodie felt at ease. The team was relaxed and content. It was a good few hours of bonding.

And then Bodie's phone rang.

He stared at the screen, feeling a little trickle of foreboding. 'It's Jack Pantera,' he said. 'I wonder what he wants.'

He answered the call. 'Hello?'

'Hey, it's me. Are you all together?'

'Yeah, we're chilling in the hotel lobby. What's up, mate?'

'Good. I've been keeping my ear to the ground. Anything the Salamander does, I've heard about it. Did you stop the robbery last night?'

Bodie hadn't told Pantera about it yet. He said, 'We certainly did. Mission accomplished.'

'Damn.'

'What do you mean by that?'

'I mean *damn*. The Salamander has gone absolutely apeshit. He's vowing revenge on whoever foiled his plans. He's gonna chase your asses to the ends of the earth.'

Bodie swallowed. 'That doesn't sound good.' The others looked at him.

'It's a living nightmare, Guy. The Salamander is one bad dude. When he wants something, he gets it. And he's on his way personally to Cairo right now.'

'And now he wants us.'

'He's demanding information, and he'll get it. The

job was a year in the planning. It's taken vast resources. You stepped in at the wrong moment. He wants you.'

'Damn.' The entire team was looking worried now, hearing only Bodie's side of the conversation.

'I'm not so sure he'll find us,' Bodie said.

'He'll backtrack. His sources are excellent. And his team saw you all. You're pretty notorious in the field of relic hunting.'

'They're gonna find us,' Bodie realised.

'Sooner or later, yes.'

'And we don't want a master criminal breathing down our necks forever.'

'You don't want this heat.'

Bodie thanked Pantera for the heads up and ended the call. He looked around at his team, told them the bad news. Smiling faces turned to glum facades. For a while, nobody said anything.

'We have to decide what to do about this,' Bodie said eventually.

'What can we do?' Heidi said. 'The Salamander wants us dead. It's not like we can find him and kill him first.'

'We could do that,' Cassidy said.

'We're not soldiers,' Bodie said. 'That's not what we do. And besides, we wouldn't get close. Imagine the security.'

'We can't ignore this,' Yasmine said.

'Nobody's ignoring it,' Bodie said. 'We're talking it through.'

'Maybe he won't find us,' Reilly said. 'It's not like we broadcasted our identities when we were searching.'

'But the bad guys got a look at us,' Bodie said. 'A good luck. And if one of our grasses speaks up, that links us to the search. Yes, I guess it's possible that he'll never find us, but can we take that chance?'

'We'd be looking over our shoulders forever,' Lucie said.

'I don't want that,' Bodie said. 'But I'm finding it hard to come up with an alternative.'

'The trouble is we have been famous,' Heidi said. 'We've been on the news. And, knowing us, we'll be famous again. If we find something in the future. That would draw undue attention.'

'Even five years down the line, he'd still be waiting.' Jemma said.

The team discussed it all afternoon. When evening announced its presence through the windows, they were still discussing it. Sitting there, they all felt exposed and uneasy, and knew it was a feeling that was unlikely to go away. Quite the opposite. The Salamander had an extensive network and, for now, it was all pointed their way.

They ate an evening meal sitting at the same table. None of them really tasted it. The happy feelings had long since evaporated. Now it was an endless circle of edgy discussion about what to do next.

'Very few people know where we live,' Cassidy said. 'Where we hang out. We're not known locally. The world is a big place. Could the Salamander really pin us down? Plus, we'd see him coming. We're pretty good at what we do.'

'I think it's a problem that needs nipping in the bud now,' Bodie said. 'Right at the source. Let's put it all behind us.'

'But how do we do that?' Jemma asked.

It was a dilemma they'd been skirting around all afternoon. But a small possibility had been growing in Bodie's mind, the kernel of a plan.

'It's risky,' he said. 'Highly risky. But I have a solution.'

The others all stopped eating and turned to him. 'What plan?' Yasmine asked.

'We let the Salamander find us.'

They stared as if he was mad. Their mouths dropped open. Before anyone could speak out, Bodie continued.

'We leave breadcrumbs so he can find us. Subtle enough so he doesn't think we've left them on purpose.'

'But we don't want him to find us,' Reilly said.

'Oh, yes we do,' Bodie said. 'Because we'll be waiting for him. Just think. He comes with his team, hunts us down. Only we're all set up and ready and know exactly what we need to do. The Salamander will never see it coming, and it'll give us a big advantage.'

'It's risky as all hell,' Reilly said. 'You're planning on fighting him? Taking him down?'

'It's that or we spend the rest of our lives waiting for him to find us,' Bodie said. 'I don't see any other alternative.'

The team thought about it, rolled it over, and eventually came up with the same conclusion. They really had no choice. Of course, there were many unknowns. But all they could do was prepare as well as they could.

'Let's get started,' Bodie said.

CHAPTER THIRTY ONE

They began by phoning up Jack Pantera.

Bodie told him about the plan. Even over the phone Bodie could see him wince.

'Are you kidding me?'

'No. That's what we've come up with. It's risky as fuck, I know. But what else can we do? We're not gonna hide away for the rest of our lives.'

'I get it, pal, I get it. Okay. What do you need from me?'

'A few things. First, we need a place to prepare. A big place. And then we need you to leave breadcrumbs with certain contacts that will allow the Salamander to find that place. Very subtle breadcrumbs though, Jack. We don't want him forewarned. Finally, we need a contact who can give us vests and weapons and comms.'

'Crap, Guy, you're going to war?'

'What else can we do?'

'The Salamander will be coming to kill you,' Pantera admitted. 'He's said it a dozen times already. He's gearing up for death. You're his biggest project at the moment.'

'That's why we need to be well prepared. All of us. We need the best gear you can get. And we need to be situated in this place as soon as possible. We need to familiarise ourselves with it intimately.'

'I understand. I'll start working on it right away.'

'Do you have any more info on the Salamander?'

'Apart from the fact that you're his number one pet project? No. All I know is he's headed for Cairo with a crack team. Maybe he's hoping to pick up the pieces there. It won't happen if I don't get started, though.'

Bodie got the hint and let him go. He looked at the others. 'Pantera's gonna do it,' he said. 'When he finds a place, we'll have to move out right away. It'll need preparing. And some of us will need to pick up our new gear.'

It was a tense waiting game. They couldn't actually do anything yet, and they had so much to do. Anxiety bore down on them like a thick blanket. It was one thing doing battle when you were in the thick of a mission, when it came out of the blue. It was quite another preparing and inviting it.

Pantera called back within the hour. 'I've got you a house that's built like a castle,' he said.

'What?'

'Yeah, it's on the outskirts of Cairo. Some rich guy liked castles and built himself one. Even has the suits of armour inside. Anyway, he went insolvent, lost the house and moved away. Place has been abandoned ever since.'

'It sounds big enough,' Bodie said. 'Let's have the address. Are there neighbours?'

'Not close. It's a big estate.'

'Sounds perfect.'

Bodie wrote down the address. Next, Pantera gave

them a place and the name of a man who could provide them with weapons, bulletproof vests and comms and other paraphernalia. He'd already arranged a time to meet later that evening.

'I'm calling a few people who the Salamander knows,' he said next. 'Telling them a few tales. It will lead the Salamander right to you. So be prepared.'

'Oh, we will be,' Bodie said. 'Thanks, Jack.'

'Good luck.'

Bodie ended the call and went into leadership mode. 'We need taxis,' he said. 'We need to get to this house, break in, and make ourselves at home. Reilly, you and Cass can go get the gear. It shouldn't be a problem with Pantera's contact. After that, it's a waiting game. We'll just have to wait and see.'

The team was ready, recognising the need to be busy to fight the nerves. They packed quickly and then called taxis and left Cassidy and Reilly behind to rent a car. They couldn't exactly transport military gear in a taxi. It was a long journey to the house through the evening traffic, though it wasn't exactly far. The taxi crawled through the busy streets.

Bodie saw the approaching house before the others. He saw two turrets and a crenelated wall peering over a white wall. There was greenery and a large arched gate with a padlock and a wide gravelled driveway. The taxi dropped them off. The team looked around. It was indeed a wide open area with the only other house being far away. Jemma turned her attention to the gate and soon they were walking down the long, winding driveway with the house hidden by trees. They left the gate unlocked for Cassidy and Reilly.

Slowly, the house came into view. It wasn't exactly a castle, but it was a good representation. There was no drawbridge, but the front door was designed to look like one. The windows weren't loopholes, but the house had decorative ones at the side of every window. There were bars and crenelations along the top of the house and, as Bodie had already seen, one towering turret at each end. The drive outside the house was expansive. Bodie walked right up to the front door and let Jemma loose on the lock. Within a minute, she had the door open and was beckoning him inside.

'Let's see what we have to work with,' he said.

Immediately he saw a long, dark-panelled hallway lined with suits of armour. The armour had helmets and swords and was dusty. The hallway stretched away the length of the house. They explored, finding a dining room to the right with a long wooden table, a sitting room to the left with a few dusty old chairs, a study, a library, and a huge globe that occupied one entire corner of the library. There was an extensive kitchen still with knives and forks and plates intact. Upstairs there were six bedrooms, all with huge draped beds. Ancient shields hung on the walls. Swords decorated every room.

'Plenty of places to hide,' Heidi said. 'I like it.'

'Let's hope they get back soon with the equipment,' Bodie said.

Jemma was staring at them. 'We're really doing this?' she said. 'Inviting a killer to come to us?'

Bodie put a hand on her shoulder. 'What choice do we have?' he said. 'Sooner or later, the guy's gonna find us.'

'It feels...wrong. Waiting here for an attack.'

'I feel the same,' Bodie said. 'But what else can we do?'

They continued exploring the house. It took a while. The turrets had large round rooms on the ground floor and small bedrooms on a high top floor. Hours later, there was a noise outside. The team went quiet and then went to investigate. Nobody expected the Salamander to arrive this quickly.

It was Cassidy and Reilly, and they needed help unloading their gear. Soon the team was taking guns, bullet-proof vests, knives, a comms system, sensors, cameras and other equipment into the house. They got together in one of the main rooms.

'Choose your weapon,' Bodie said.

They spent some time sorting out the guns and knives and the spare ammo. It was a tense, fraught few hours. They set up sensors outside, so that anyone approaching would trigger a remote alarm that would buzz on their phones.

Slowly, their fortress took shape.

They chose knives and donned vests, strapped them up. They installed the cameras and trained them around the house, synced them to their phones. The more eyes they had, the better. It was a tired and hungry team that declared itself ready the next morning.

Jack Pantera called them around noon.

'I've done all I can,' he said. 'It's set up. The Salamander should be able to find you through mutual contacts.'

'Thanks Jack,' Bodie said. It felt strange thanking someone for putting them in danger.

'You're welcome, though I'm not sure I agree with what you're doing.'

'It's the only way we're ever going to get him off our backs.'

'You're gonna make a lot of noise.'

'We'll just have to hope it all happens fast and we can get away. There are no neighbours.'

'Good luck, mate.'

Jack signed off and Lucie ordered a takeout. They had pizza delivered to the house. It was a waiting game now. All the sensors worked when the pizza came, confirming their hard work. They put Cassidy on guard too whilst they sat around and ate, guns at hand. A blanket of tension enveloped them. How and when would the Salamander come?

It wasn't for the rest of the afternoon. They finished their food and talked, trying to ignore the tautness that filled them. Bodie cleaned his gun, getting used to the weapon. He didn't like guns, hated them. But this was the Salamander coming for them, and, by all accounts, he wanted to kill them.

Needs must.

Time passed. When evening fell, they put Reilly on guard. Cassidy could relax. They would change guards throughout the night.

It was a long, cold, nervous night. Still, nothing happened. The early hours felt stretched and strained. Bodie and Heidi sat up talking and, he guessed, so did the others. They didn't need to talk about what they would do when the Salamander arrived. They were well drilled. But nothing took the pressure away from those hours, nothing eased. They could talk and laugh and smile all they wanted, but the spectre of the Salamander hung over them like a looming, vicious guillotine.

And then another day dawned.

CHAPTER THIRTY TWO

Bodie and the others waited for Reilly and Jemma to drive to a shop and buy them breakfast. They couldn't all leave the house. Soon, they were eating pastries and drinking coffee and sat around whilst Heidi took watch. The food was good, but it didn't make the waiting any easier.

'It seems unfair,' Lucie said. 'That we saved the mask, but end up like this. Not only that, but nobody can help us after all we did.'

'It is unfair,' Reilly said. 'But it's all we've got. That's how life ends up sometimes.'

'I just want to get back to New York,' Lucie said. 'Back to real life.'

'We succeeded,' Bodie said with a little smile. 'Now we pay the price.'

His statement brought an end to the conversation. They ate the rest of their food and sat in silence, staring into space. It was a sombre few hours.

It was the beginning of the afternoon, and Yasmine was on watch. She stood by a fountain in the shade of a statue, watching the front gates and the road that led up to them. It was their best vantage point. Her mind was drifting when she saw movement on the road. The house was pretty isolated, so movement was something to worry about. Yasmine straightened. She saw three vehicles headed their way, large black SUVs with tinted windows. The vehicles weren't slowing down.

Yasmine jumped on the comms system immediately.

'Someone's coming,' she said. 'And they're coming fast. It's all happening right now.'

Bodie and the others jumped up and ran to their prearranged positions. Bodie took his gun out, a light Glock, and checked his pocket was full of spare ammo. He would need it, he imagined. He watched the front gates, but saw nothing for now.

Yasmine saw it all. The three vehicles stopped right outside the gates. Doors were flung open. Men ran for the gates and worked the lock. When they were open, the men ran through and the cars came on, bringing the Salamander and his men.

The cars roared down the driveway. Yasmine slipped into a hiding position that would put her behind the bad guys, hidden by a stand of trees. From there, she could pick them off one by one and they'd have no place to hide. At least, that was the idea.

The cars crunched across the gravel driveway, coming to an abrupt halt. Again, doors were flung open. Men and women jumped out, all clad in black and carrying weapons. They studied the house but did nothing else for now.

After a while, a man climbed out of the front. He was the only one not dressed in black. He wore a pale grey suit and had white hair and carried a knife that looked like a short sword. He twirled it as he addressed the house.

'Come talk to me,' he yelled. 'We should meet since you have caused me so much trouble.' The Salamander waited. He looked lithe and fit and ready to do battle. There was a gun attached to his hip.

Bodie rose from his hiding place and cracked a window. 'You'd do best to turn around and leave us alone for the rest of your life,' he said. 'We're armed and we have you all covered from multiple positions.'

'I do not care about that,' the Salamander replied. 'You embarrassed me. You hurt me. I can't let you get away with that.'

'So you'd rather die?'

'It is all about honour,' the Salamander cried out. 'It is now known far and wide that I failed. The first failure of my life. And I wanted that mask very, very badly. I have wanted it for years. *You* stopped me getting it. That plan was developed for a year.'

Bodie would not apologise. He stayed low. 'You're a damn criminal,' he said. 'The right thing is to stop you.'

'And now you will pay for your actions.'

'So will you,' Bodie assured him.

The Salamander stepped back and looked like he was about to order the attack, but then his face grew thoughtful and he came forward again. 'One thing,' he said. 'I may not know your identities, but I tracked you down here. Remember that. You will never be safe from me.'

Bodie hid a smile. He knew that already. He didn't answer and readied his weapon. It was all about to go down. He could see Yasmine standing in the garden, mostly concealed. The others were all at the best positions, both upstairs and downstairs and ready to fight.

The Salamander walked behind his car and shouted once more as he walked, shouted over his shoulder. 'I have killed many men and women,' he said. 'This will be the most pleasurable.'

And his people opened fire. It was an assault to the ears. Bullets laced the air, flying into brickwork and wooden frames and shattering glass. Bodie could only duck as the barrage began. Many of the shots were centred on his window, being the most obvious target. He was glad to hear his own team firing down from unobserved positions upstairs.

To his right, Lucie popped up and fired her own weapon. To his left, Jemma did the same. Everyone else was upstairs. Bodie didn't dare raise his own hand in case he caught a bullet. The noise was tremendous. Bullets now pinged off the cars too, shattering side windows and embedding into the metalwork.

From the treeline, Yasmine stepped out. She had a clear line of sight to the vehicles and the men crouching behind them. She raised her weapon.

And fired. She had to be quick because they'd soon realise where she was. Her first bullet took a man in the back, only knocking him down because he was wearing a vest. Her second bullet smashed through a man's head. Blood exploded all over the car. The men and women around him didn't necessarily think they were being hit from behind – the bullet could have come from the house.

Yasmine's third shot winged a woman, who dropped her gun and fell to her knees. Her fourth killed another man, and then she just had time for a fifth, which missed everybody and smashed into the vehicle.

The woman had caught on when she fell. She turned around, saw Yasmine, and yelled out a warning. People span and started firing as Yasmine ducked back behind a tree. Now she would have to move.

She'd planned her route earlier that day. She slipped between trees, soon finding another vantage position. When she looked back at the vehicles, one man had been sent to despatch her and he was out in the open running towards the place she had been. She took aim and fired off a shot. The bullet hit his chest, knocking him off his feet. He lay on the ground, trying to shake off the impact. Yasmine lined him up again, but a shot from near the cars made her take cover. They had seen her again.

She crouched and peeked back around the tree. The man was on his knees. She aimed carefully. She fired, but another bullet hit her tree. Her aim was off. She hit her guy in the thigh, but that put him back on the ground, writhing. He was out of action and bleeding heavily.

Yasmine ran for her next vantage point.

Inside the house, Bodie brought his gun up and fired off a few shots. He had seen the damage Yasmine had done. The vehicles were riddled with bullets now, as was the house. Bodie couldn't see the Salamander but, in lulls in the shooting, he heard the man's voice urging violence.

Right then, a man climbed into one of the cars and started the engine. Bodie frowned. *What?* He didn't have to wonder for long. The guy drove the vehicle closer to the house, giving his team better access. Now the vehicle was right next to the front door. A difficult angle for Lucie who was situated down there.

She tagged a man running for the door. She wounded another. Then, cover fire rained on her window so she was forced to pull back. She hunkered down as glass shattered over her, a few shards piercing her clothing and staying there. Bodie then concentrated his own fire on the people who were targeting Lucie.

He forced them back down.

The Salamander popped up occasionally, a SIG Sauer clasped in one hand. He seemed to rejoice in firing it at the upstairs windows, trying to take someone out. He didn't look wary or worried about getting shot, just looked happy to be there. Bodie knew there would be no quarter offered by the Salamander.

The minutes flashed by. The bullets kept coming. Bodie knew they were lucky to be in an isolated position. Hopefully, nobody else could hear all this. He heard someone smashing on the locked front door and leaned out to take a shot.

Almost got his head blown off. A bullet flew by just a few inches to his left, impacted the window frame, and sent a shard slamming into his temple. Bodie winced. He was going to have to cover the front door.

He ducked back and ran that way now, saw the front door. It was shuddering in its frame as people launched themselves at it. Should he fire through it, or would that weaken it? One thing was for sure – it would send those on the other side scurrying.

Bodie fired three quick shots. There were two yells

and a grunt. The door stopped shuddering. Bodie crept back into cover just in time, as someone opened fire on the door from the other side. Bullets smashed through the wood, sending bits of the door into the hallway. One of the suits of armour clanged as a bullet hit it, the sound incongruous in the circumstances. A sword was hit and fell off the wall. Bodie was hiding to the left of the door and now leaned out, firing again. More of the door disintegrated.

CHAPTER THIRTY THREE

Upstairs, Cassidy, Heidi and Reilly had their own vantage points. They had a good view down on the cars and quite an advantage with their angles. They broke the glass, leaned out and fired down, keeping the bad guys pinned behind their vehicles. Cassidy shot a foot that was poking out and heard the guy's scream. She shot another in the elbow. Only when the enemy teamed up and fired all at once did she have to take cover. Her window was riddled with lead, much of the wood hanging off. When the barrage subsided, she chanced another look and started firing again. Her bullets hit glass and metal and tyres. She tried to tag the Salamander, but he was too well hidden. In fact, he almost tagged her on one of his brief attacks. She was kneeling on a chair to see properly out of the window, and his attack forced her to fall off it onto her side. Cassidy could already feel the bruise forming.

It was pure mayhem. A scene from hell. The bad guys were now concentrating more on the front door, trying to get it open. But as they aimed more at the door, it started to disintegrate even further. There was now a large hole in the centre, probably big enough for a person to fit through. Of course, nobody wanted to be first through because they knew they'd get shot.

Bodie deterred them with harsh fire. He saw through the hole to the outside, saw that he shot another guy in the head. This sent the man slamming back against the vehicle, its shattered windows now covered in his blood.

The relic hunters were well hidden in the house. It was a good refuge. But now the enemy was getting anxious and was determined to get inside. They looked for other routes to enter and, unfortunately, there were many windows along the front — too many for the relic hunters to man.

Yasmine crawled through the grass, now in another special vantage point. She aimed for the people at the door, shooting a woman before they ducked into cover. There was a second when she had the Salamander in her sights but, when she fired, he luckily ducked out of the way. A woman had been sent to despatch her, and now Yasmine saw her sprinting the short distance between them.

Yasmine aimed her weapon and fired. For once, her aim was off, the bullet flying wide. The woman was fast. She had short black hair and a determined face. She carried her own gun and fired at Yasmine, forcing her to duck behind a tree.

Yasmine could only wait as bullets impacted the trunk. Then the woman hit her hiding place and came around, weapon raised. Yasmine grabbed her gun arm and forced it high. The weapon discharged, shooting into the boughs above. Yasmine kneed the woman in the gut, tried to sweep her off her feet. The woman ignored the blow and held fast, trying to bring her gun to bear.

Yasmine now had hold of both of the woman's hands. She swung her around, backed her hard into the tree. She held fast to both wrists, keeping the gun pointed high. Her own gun was trapped at the woman's side, ineffectual.

The women fought for their lives. Yasmine brought her head down hard, breaking the woman's nose. She staggered. Her grip weakened. Yasmine didn't let up. She used her knee again, felt some energy leave the other woman.

She used her head again. The woman half-slumped. Yasmine managed to get her gun pointed into the woman's midriff and pulled the trigger. There was a slightly muffled blast and then the woman staggered away, shot point blank in the vest. She cringed.

Yasmine shot her in the head, sent her flying back off her feet. The woman hit the tree and slithered down it, dead.

Yasmine turned back to the battle, breathing heavily.

Bodie saw two men running for the door. They smashed through it, shattering it to pieces. They rolled when they hit the floor, came up with their guns in their hands. Bodie had already sighted on them. When they came up, he shot one in the face and the other in the neck. Both men died instantly, but now the door was just a wide gap.

With only him to protect it.

Now a man and a woman approached the door, firing constantly. Bodie couldn't risk the wall of lead. He stayed back. The man and woman were in the house, still shooting. Bodie waited for them to draw level with his hiding place. He didn't step out. He went prone on the floor and shot at their ankles. The man yelled out, struck. The woman hesitated. Bodie leapt out and grabbed her hand. He grappled with her gun whilst shooting down at the man with the bullet in his ankle. Two battles at the same time. The man was distracted by agony, but was still trying to bring his gun to bear. The woman had been distracted but was now fighting hard, trying to get Bodie off balance.

He fired two bullets into the man, unable to aim at anything but his vest. The man groaned and then squirmed in pain. Bodie yanked at the woman's gun hand, pulling it hard. She staggered to the right.

Bodie shot the groaning man in the head.

By now, another two men were running through the shattered door.

Bodie head-butted the woman harder than he'd ever done it in his life, then turned and ran. He was outnumbered. The enemy was forcing its way into the house.

Bodie found another place to hide behind the fridge. He upended it, watched it crash to the floor. He leaned over it, gun aimed.

The bloody-faced woman and two men ran straight for him. He fired as fast as he was able. The bullets hit them hard, knocking them sideways. One man died. The woman, who seemed blessed with luck, took a bullet to the side and kept coming.

Bodie rose to meet her again. She missed her stride and tumbled over the fridge, rolling under him. Bodie swung to shoot her, but saw her gun aimed at his face.

'Not this time,' she said and pulled the trigger.

As she did, her head exploded. It was Lucie, firing from inside the main room, seeing Bodie's plight. It had been a great shot. When she died, the woman's trigger finger flexed, and the shot went wide.

Bodie didn't have time to thank Lucie. The other man was already on him. He'd lost his gun and now came swinging wildly, trying to put Bodie off. It worked. Bodie took the impact of the man's attack, staggering. He was bruised and bloody and tired. He went down to one knee. The other man stood over him, fists raised like a club. He brought them down hard like a sledgehammer.

Bodie just fell to the floor, under the man's range. He still had his gun. He fired it now, hitting the man's left knee, and heard him yell. When he fell to his knees, Bodie shot him in the head.

'We've lost the front door,' he yelled over the comms. 'They'll be in the house soon.'

He scrambled back, looking for more cover. The enemy was swarming through the front door and entering the house. Bodie couldn't count them all. At least six. He watched through a window and the door that led into the hallway, seeing their shapes and figures, watching them run past.

There was a back stairway up there, but Heidi, Cassidy and Reilly were aware of it.

Bodie concentrated on those running from the cars to the front door. They were out in the open for at least seven seconds. Bodie hit two, who rolled out of sight. He wasn't sure if they were dead or just injured.

From outside, he heard more ominous sounds.

The crash of windows breaking along the ground floor. People were entering there too. The relic hunters couldn't defend everything, and it was a big place.

Upstairs, Cassidy knew they were coming. She'd heard Bodie's message, but she also had a sensor back there at the top of the stairs. Her phone buzzed now, and she knew it was a warning.

She turned away from the window, went to the door. She had a good line of sight along the hallway. He saw three running figures, gave them time to approach. She wanted all of them. She knew Reilly and Heidi would also be taking aim.

Cassidy let them come. It wasn't easy, letting them get closer and closer. The men were bulky in their vests, and one, oddly, wore a mask. They cleared a few rooms as they came, becoming increasingly stealthy.

When they were close enough, Cassidy opened fire. Her first bullet caught the man at the rear in the head, took him down. Her second bullet glanced off another man's head, again knocking him to the floor. Her third swiftly fired bullet missed because her target was already firing back. Cassidy felt an impact on the doorjamb at her side. She ducked lower, kept firing. Her shots hit the third person in the chest and that person also went down. Cassidy saw Reilly emerge from his room, run over to the felled person, and finish it. There were no more warnings from the sensor.

Cassidy ran back to the window. She leaned out, fired down at the remaining men. There weren't many hiding behind the cars now. Some were in the house. But she could still see the Salamander in his grey suit, flanked by two guys. She tried to shoot him now, but the angle was too narrow.

With people in the house, maybe it was time to leave the windows now and start a search of her own.

She jumped on the comms. 'Gonna start going through the house.'

'Got you,' Bodie came back.

'Me too,' Reilly said. 'Don't shoot me.'

'I'll stay by the window,' Heidi said. 'Try to keep the remaining few at bay.'

'Maybe if they lose enough men, they'll leave,' Yasmine said.

'Hasn't worked so far,' Bodie said.

Cassidy slipped out into the hall. Her sensor went off. Immediately, she ducked and saw a figure rushing towards her. She raised her gun. Too late. The woman was right on top of her. She rose, met her with a hard punch to the face. She had a handgun and twisted it towards her as she staggered left. Cassidy chopped at it and then grabbed the wrist, forcing it away. The woman punched out with her free hand, striking Cassidy's temple. Cassidy saw stars, but didn't let it deter her. She grappled hard, took another punch, and then blocked a third. She struck back, then flung her opponent around, trying to loosen her grip. The woman slipped. Cassidy saw an opportunity. With both her hands engaged, she used her boot. She kicked down at the woman's knee, saw the joint buckle. The woman cried out. Cassidy wrenched her gun free and then shot the woman in the head.

She slithered away. Cassidy didn't slow down. She

crept to the head of the stairs and then started down.

Bodie slunk through the house, looking for the enemy. They were here somewhere, but they were thinning out and would be harder to find. He waited by a corner, then peered around it.

And almost froze in shock as he came face to face with a bearded man. Both opponents stared at each other for half a second before reacting. Bodie then punched out, striking his enemy in the throat. He brought the gun up at the same time, but not too far, this time aiming for the man's legs. He fired. The bullet punched into the man's meaty thigh.

The man was just as quick. Reeling from the throat punch, he lifted his own gun and fired. The bullet smashed into Bodie's vest, knocking him backwards. Pain flared through him. The impact site was a throbbing mess. The man shouted and went down to one knee. His gun was still aimed at Bodie, but the pain in his leg was almost too much to bear.

His head was now level with Bodie's gun.

Bodie had the presence of mind to finish him off. He gasped for a few seconds, and then the pain started to abate. He would have a fantastic bruise later.

His job wasn't done yet. He crept into the new room and started across, searching for the enemy.

Outside, Yasmine decided to take out the Salamander.

She had seen several people enter the house, had tried to shoot them but missed all but one. Now, she moved to the edge of the treeline and looked towards the man. He was crouched behind one of the vehicles in a kind of dip in the ground, just below eye level. He had two men with him.

Yasmine guessed the distance. It was about twenty yards, but it was twenty yards of empty space. Nowhere to hide. She watched. The Salamander appeared to be prone, doing nothing. As she watched, something happened.

His bodyguards rose, and he was between them. As one, they started for the house. Yasmine lined them up in her sights. She opened fire. Her shot hit one of the bodyguards, spinning him around and smashing him back into the car, denting its side. Then, the remaining bodyguard and the Salamander started running. Yasmine fired again, but her shots went wide.

'Salamander is in the house,' she said through the comms. 'Repeat, Salamander is in the house.'

Now there was nobody between her and the house. Yasmine ran hard, heading for the front door.

Inside, Bodie decided the best way to end this was to take the Salamander out. He retraced his footsteps now, headed for the front door. Soon, he was approaching and then saw the Salamander pass through the hallway ahead. He didn't have time to shoot, but he increased his pace.

He heard gunshots from various parts of the house, one from close by, probably Jemma. He reached a corner and peered around.

The Salamander and a bodyguard were far ahead, walking down the wide passage. Bodie stepped out and crept after them. Every step, he was conscious of no hiding places. If they turned, they would have a free shot. But then, so would he.

Bodie stole along in their wake. When he got close enough, he would fire, but they were too far away. He was closing the gap. Any second now. Any second...

There was a sudden movement. To his right. An arm came out of an open doorway and smashed into his head.

Bodie went down.

CHAPTER THIRTY FOUR

The blow didn't disorient him, it just sent him crashing to the floor. He hit the wood hard, then swivelled in place, turning onto his back. Looking up, he saw a grizzled face and the barrel of a gun.

The man opened fire first.

Another shot to the vest. The man was rushed. Bodie felt the impact and ignored the pain. He fired a shot of his own, hitting the man's body, sending him staggering back. Without pause, he fired two more shots, this time into the man's legs. He fell to the floor and Bodie shot him in the head.

Looked ahead. The Salamander was gone.

He cursed, then picked himself up and tried to ignore the burgeoning pain that filled his chest. Slowly, steadily, he limped along the passage. He knew there was a kitchen at the far end, and it was probably there where the Salamander had gone. He hurried along as fast as he could.

More gunshots through the house. Then Cassidy's voice came on the comms.

'I'm not seeing anyone. Have we got 'em all?'

'Same here,' Reilly said. 'I don't see anyone.'

'The Salamander and at least one other are on the ground floor,' Bodie said. 'I'm tracking them now.'

'Coming to you,' Cassidy said.

'Headed for the kitchen,' he returned.

Bodie now approached the kitchen door. It stood wide open. He waited and listened for half a minute and then peered inside. And took a blow to the face. The bodyguard had been waiting for him. The strike smashed into his nose, almost breaking it. Involuntary tears filled his eyes. He reeled back, arms akimbo. The bodyguard stepped around the frame and brought up a gun, took a moment to adjust so he was aiming at Bodie's head.

It was the moment Bodie needed. He stepped in, kicked the man's gun arm and watched the weapon fly away. He threw a punch at the man's face, cracked his jaw. The bodyguard wasn't deterred. He pulled out a long knife and jabbed it at Bodie in a swift motion. The thrust was so quick Bodie couldn't get out of the way. It hit his vest, adding to the pain, but at least saving his life.

Bodie brought the gun up now. He fired as he did so. The bullet flew underneath the man's arm. Missing him completely. Bodie faced the knife again, this time squirming aside as it came at him. His finger was on the trigger of his gun and he fired again, twice.

The first shot hit the guy in his vest. The second clicked on empty.

The bodyguard was swaying back, creased in pain. Bodie dropped his gun for now, knowing he wouldn't have time to slap in another mag. He drew a knife of his own and slashed it at the guard's throat.

The guy lurched away. Bodie's knife almost split

the skin, an inch away. He recovered and came back with a strike of his own. Bodie let the thrust travel between his arm and his ribs, then trapped the arm and threw his knife to his left hand.

Now he had a free strike.

He jammed the knife into the bodyguard's arm, withdrew it, and stood back. The man swayed, holding his wound. Bodie stepped in then and cut the man's neck, mindful to jump away from the spray of blood.

As he did so, the Salamander appeared in Cassidy's firm grip.

'Let go of me,' the man cried. 'I will kill you all for this.'

'You've already tried,' Cassidy growled. 'And failed.'

Bodie spoke briefly into the comms. 'Sweep the house from top to bottom. Make sure we got them all.'

He walked up to the Salamander. 'We have you now and could kill you. Are you going to call this vendetta off?'

'I will never let you live.'

'It's either that, or we kill you now.'

The Salamander glared at him and said nothing.

'He's never going to stop,' Cassidy said. 'We can't let him walk away.'

'I will make sure you all die. I am the Salamander. You can't kill me. I could destroy any of you.'

'You could?' Cassidy looked up for the challenge.

Bodie faced a tough dilemma. He couldn't just execute this man. But he couldn't let him go because, eventually, the Salamander would find them and they'd face the same situation. Right then, he heard a gunshot in the house and assumed another enemy had been flushed out.

'We're in the kitchen,' Bodie said through the comms.

There was a heavy silence. Cassidy held the Salamander tight. Bodie focused on the man, watching him closely.

And that was why he didn't hear movement behind him. One minute he was standing there, the next he was falling to his knees, pain exploding in his head, blood running down his face.

Bodie fell to the floor, half unconscious.

A man stepped through the door, all clad in black. Cassidy saw a thin, hard-faced enemy with a chin like a blade. He had a gun in one hand and was aiming it at Bodie's head.

Cassidy acted faster than she ever had in her life. She threw the Salamander aside, raised her gun and fired. Her bullet smashed into her opponent just as he squeezed his own trigger. The man flew back, face erased, and his own shot went wide. Bodie groaned on the floor.

Cassidy gasped in relief.

But then the Salamander attacked, catching her off guard. He whirled like a dervish, kicking out. His foot caught her gun hand and sent the weapon flying. The Salamander continued his spin, kicking out again. This blow caught her across the face and sent her reeling.

Cassidy crashed into the large fridge head first. Black spots danced before her eyes. The Salamander didn't relent. He leapt forward, leading with a knee that just missed her nose. He struck down at her with stiffened fingers. One hand struck luckily just above her eyes, the other into a nerve cluster at her shoulder. Cassidy screamed. She twisted away, disorientated.

The Salamander slipped out a knife.

He rushed in, slicing the weapon at Cassidy's face. Cassidy was hurt, and she was dazed, but she was also a seasoned, trained fighter who had fought in harsh battles all her life. She dug deep. She flung up a hand, deflecting the knife. It cut her wrist. Blood flooded out, falling between her and the Salamander like rain. He thrust again. Cassidy twisted away and kicked out. Her feet slammed into his knees, unbalancing him. He stepped away. Cassidy jerked herself upright and stood before him, hunched over.

'Come on then,' she said. 'Do your worst.'

The Salamander attacked with the knife. His thrust came at her midriff, then changed halfway through and went up at her chin. Cassidy was ready for it. She caught the wrist in midair, just inches from her flesh, and held on to it. Though her body throbbed in agony, she met the Salamander face to face, stared him right in the eyes.

She broke the wrist, making him scream.

To his credit, he pulled away from her then, performing another spin kick. This time, she was ready. She ducked underneath it and punched out hard at his groin. The Salamander folded, falling into a moaning heap.

Cassidy stood over him now with her own knife. The best thing to do would be to end it all right now, put an end to the vendetta.

But she couldn't do it. Not in cold blood. Couldn't put an end to the madness.

She stood there swaying, still in agony. Her nerve endings were on fire. She would calm soon, she knew, and then she would tie the Salamander up.

There was a sudden movement. The Salamander shifted. His good arm came from underneath his body, holding a gun. It was pointed right at her. She had nowhere to go and could only stare at it.

'You utter bastard,' she said.

And then the shot rang out, echoing loudly through the room. Cassidy flinched and fell back.

The shot had not hit her. *What the hell?* It took her several moments to realise that the shot had come from Bodie's gun. From the floor, he had fired at the Salamander, shot him in the head. He had saved Cassidy's life. He looked up at her now and rose to his knees, gave her a thumbs up.

'Good job,' he said.

Cassidy felt her knees wobble. She fell to the floor, overwhelmed. She'd thought she was dead, even heard the gunshot. But it hadn't happened. She lived to fight another day.

It took a while, but soon the others came into the kitchen. The house had been swept and then swept again. There were no more of the Salamander's people within. Now, all that remained was for the relic hunters to get the hell out. It had been a terrible, deadly experience, but they had survived.

Albeit with a plethora of wounds. They quickly bandaged Cassidy's wrist, and then headed for their own vehicle. Soon, they were driving away.

The sun shone like a beacon of hope above.

Bodie latched on to it and watched it all the way.

CHAPTER THIRTY FIVE

It was a battered, bruised and exhausted team that landed in New York two days later. They brought none of their equipment and little luggage and all tried to sleep on the plane. For most, it was impossible. The flight was bumpy and noisy and filled with excited holiday makers. Not to mention the memories of battle that swirled through their minds.

They disembarked and made their way through the crowds around security and in the arrivals lounge. They were still hyped, still hugely affected by everything that had happened. What they had done to the Salamander's team did not sit easy with them, and the whole trauma of the battle would never dissipate.

They headed out of the airport and found a restaurant to crash in. Nobody wanted to go home yet. They wanted to unwind in each other's company, not alone. They sat down and, first, ordered shots of brandy all around.

'To us,' Bodie said, raising his glass. 'And a job well done.'

The team drank, emptying their glasses. Bodie stared from face to face, seeing haunted eyes all around. It would not be easy, the next weeks and months. Maybe they would find something to keep them distracted.

They ordered starters and mains and sat back, now with larger drinks. They tried to keep the chatter inconsequential, away from the subject of the Salamander. But they were happy about the heist they'd foiled, and that subject came up often.

At one point, Jack Pantera called them to say he'd reenforced the threat against the sacred funerary mask, and they had to tell him that the threat of the Salamander had been negated. It was a sombre conversation, and it brought them down. But when Pantera signed off, they resumed their conversations and their meal and forgot their troubles.

At least for a little while.

'It was such a good interlude in our lives,' Lucie was saying. 'Saving the mask, I mean. It was worthy.'

'Of the relic hunters,' Bodie said. 'We did a good, creditable job.'

'I'm so glad we did it,' Lucie was enthused.

'And now we're back to where we were,' Heidi said. 'No agency, no jobs, no cash-flow. This could be square one...again.'

'We can work on that,' Bodie said quietly. 'It's just a matter of time before we can start up the agency and the jobs come rolling in.'

'It's been months,' Heidi said.

'Have faith,' Bodie held her hand. 'It will happen.'

Cassidy leaned forward. She was aching and throbbing and moving as little as possible. She said, 'I have to say it was a job well done. And, yes, a worthy one. We saved that relic. We helped save the museum. And nobody even knows it was us.'

'I wonder if they've found the bodies at the house,' Yasmine said. They had erased any evidence that they were there, including all the cameras and sensors.

'I don't want to think about that,' Lucie said. 'Ever again.'

Bodie silently agreed. He took some time to eat and drink and listened to the flow of conversation. It was a good flow; the team was easing back into real life. It was a testament to the human condition that you could heal so quickly, a testament to the state of mind of his team. To him, it was everything.

The evening turned around them, and they did not know what was coming next. They did not know where they would end up. All they knew was that the future was uncertain, unknown, in the balance.

The world turned around the relic hunters, and whatever fate awaited them, it would come for them soon enough.

THE END

I hope you enjoyed the latest Relic Hunters tale and liked the different direction. It was a fun book to write and research, and left me wanting to do more! It's always fun to join up with Bodie and the crew. Next up, will be a new release around July or August. Thanks for reading!

Other Books by David Leadbeater:

Blood Requiem

The Matt Drake Series
A constantly evolving, action-packed romp based in the escapist action-adventure genre:

The Bones of Odin (Matt Drake #1)
The Blood King Conspiracy (Matt Drake #2)
The Gates of Hell (Matt Drake 3)
The Tomb of the Gods (Matt Drake #4)
Brothers in Arms (Matt Drake #5)
The Swords of Babylon (Matt Drake #6)
Blood Vengeance (Matt Drake #7)
Last Man Standing (Matt Drake #8)
The Plagues of Pandora (Matt Drake #9)
The Lost Kingdom (Matt Drake #10)
The Ghost Ships of Arizona (Matt Drake #11)
The Last Bazaar (Matt Drake #12)
The Edge of Armageddon (Matt Drake #13)
The Treasures of Saint Germain (Matt Drake #14)
Inca Kings (Matt Drake #15)
The Four Corners of the Earth (Matt Drake #16)
The Seven Seals of Egypt (Matt Drake #17)
Weapons of the Gods (Matt Drake #18)
The Blood King Legacy (Matt Drake #19)
Devil's Island (Matt Drake #20)
The Fabergé Heist (Matt Drake #21)
Four Sacred Treasures (Matt Drake #22)
The Sea Rats (Matt Drake #23)
Blood King Takedown (Matt Drake #24)
Devil's Junction (Matt Drake #25)
Voodoo soldiers (Matt Drake #26)
The Carnival of Curiosities (Matt Drake #27)

Theatre of War (Matt Drake #28)
Shattered Spear (Matt Drake #29)
Ghost Squadron (Matt Drake #30)
A Cold Day in Hell (Matt Drake #31)
The Winged Dagger (Matt Drake #32)
Two Minutes to Midnight (Matt Drake #33)
The Devil's Reaper (Matt Drake#34)
The Dark Tsar (Matt Drake #35)
The Hellhound Scrolls (Matt Drake #36)

The Alicia Myles Series
Aztec Gold (Alicia Myles #1)
Crusader's Gold (Alicia Myles #2)
Caribbean Gold (Alicia Myles #3)
Chasing Gold (Alicia Myles #4)
Galleon's Gold (Alicia Myles #5)
Hawaiian Gold (Alicia Myles #6)

The Torsten Dahl Thriller Series
Stand Your Ground (Dahl Thriller #1)

The Relic Hunters Series
The Relic Hunters (Relic Hunters #1)
The Atlantis Cipher (Relic Hunters #2)
The Amber Secret (Relic Hunters #3)
The Hostage Diamond (Relic Hunters #4)
The Rocks of Albion (Relic Hunters #5)
The Illuminati Sanctum (Relic Hunters #6)
The Illuminati Endgame (Relic Hunters #7)
The Atlantis Heist (Relic Hunters #8)
The City of a Thousand Ghosts (Relic Hunters #9)
Hierarchy of Madness (Relic Hunters #10)
The Contest (Relic Hunters #11)
The Maestro's Treasure (Relic Hunters #12)

The Joe Mason Series
The Vatican Secret (Joe Mason #1)
The Demon Code (Joe Mason #2)
The Midnight Conspiracy (Joe Mason #3)
The Babylon Plot (Joe Mason #4)
The Traitor's Gold (Joe Mason #5)
The Angel Deception (Joe Mason #6)

The Rogue Series
Rogue (Book One)

The Disavowed Series:
The Razor's Edge (Disavowed #1)
In Harm's Way (Disavowed #2)
Threat Level: Red (Disavowed #3)

The Chosen Few Series
Chosen (The Chosen Trilogy #1)
Guardians (The Chosen Trilogy #2)
Heroes (The Chosen Trilogy #3)

Short Stories
Walking with Ghosts (A short story)
A Whispering of Ghosts (A short story)

DAVID LEADBEATER

All genuine comments are very welcome at:

davidleadbeater2011@hotmail.co.uk

Twitter: @dleadbeater2011

Visit David's website for the latest news and information:
davidleadbeater.com

Printed in Dunstable, United Kingdom